SOUTH TEXAS DRAG

Tony Molina

STORY MERCHANT BOOKS

STORY MERCHANT BOOKS · LOS ANGELES · 2016

South Texas Drag

ISBN-13: 978-0-9969908-8-2

Story Merchant Books
400 S. Burnside Ave. #11B,
Los Angeles, CA 90036
http://www.storymerchant.com/books.html

Interior Design: Danielle Canfield
Editor: Lisa Cerasoli
Cover: Claire Moore

SOUTH
TEXAS
DRAG

THIS BOOK IS DEDICATED TO my father, Antonio Molina, a lifelong educator and community leader. He inspired me to strive past my own limits, look at life with care, and instilled a responsibility to leave the world a better place.

SOUTH
TEXAS
DRAG

1

GOOD MORNING

My eyes open and I can feel the heat of the day. It's not even 9:00 a.m. The air in South Texas is like a hot skillet, pressing you down into the dirt. It's all we can really count on in South Texas, the heat.

Chingado, what did I drink last night? The best way to tell if I had a good time is to see how many wadded-up dollar bills I have in my jeans pocket. As I sit up on the bed and pull my pockets inside out, a pile of wrinkled bills tumbles to the floor. All I can say is, I made it home and I'm still alive. These are the days I wish I still lived back with my jefita. I would have my clothes cleaned and refinando my mom's cooking.

Living at home with the life I have was not the best idea. That's why I had to leave her. Knowing about my actions would only break my jefita's heart. If my jefito were still alive, I wouldn't be running and gunning the smuggler's life. He was a strong man, with character and a pair to go with it. My tio never tangled with him. A lousy heart attack precipitated his early departure from this world, and made me an open target.

I was fifteen and the bills were racking up, so I had only one place to turn. What is a brother to do but cowboy up? In South Texas, your opportunities are slim and none. Maybe I'm not the man my dad wished me to be, but I keep his words and lessons close to the vest, like a good hand in poker. I'm not a bad man, but a good man having to do bad things to other bad people—people who would bury you in a shallow grave for lousy paper.

Where this entire drug running business started was in a backroom of good people suffering to survive in a harsh land, where this was the big, easy prize, like winning the Lotto. And how many lotto winners do you know have cursed the day they won? I only know one, and he sure as shit does, so that makes all of 'em. Nothing good comes from running drugs. Have you ever heard anything good happening when drugs or guns show up in the mix?

I am this life of drug smuggling, but I have a feeling I will tame it for the better.

I jump in the shower to shed the smoke and stale beer left by the lousy bars I love to frequent. A shower is one of the best things to do in this heat. I usually take three a day.

I get out and notice my dogs are quiet—always a good thing. There's five acres between civilization and my place. My hounds are like my security guards; I depend on them for my safety. Smartest thing I could do with times being as they are on the Texas border.

Goddam it, I scuffed my new Liberty Dallas boots. I had to call the owner of the company in Canada to find this exact pair. He was a very cool cat—a boot designer and musician. I'm the only South Texas river rat with a pair. They have longhorns on the front, with Texas stars around the barrel. In South Texas, you never try to stray too far from the norm when it comes to dress. Wrangler's Ely snap shirts and a belt buckle big enough to catch HBO with—that's pretty much my standard. I took ownership of this particular buckle after strong-arming a bar owner in Fort Worth. Some designer made them just for the restaurant. It can even open beer bottles. Really, it has an opener built in and comes in handy out in the ranches.

Fuck, where is my beeper? Under the fucking bed. How did that happen? I passed out fully clothed. Motherfucker—my uncle paged me at 5:00 a.m. This guy is not the type to be ignored or made to wait. As I'm calling him, I can feel this deep black feeling of being kicked by a horse, dead in my chest.

He answers with the deep scratchy voice of a man who has dined at hell's kitchen and went back for seconds.

"Hello, Tio. Sorry I didn't call you earlier, I...I know. I— meet you where? Why there? Everything okay? Okay. 1:00 p.m. today. I got it."

Meet my uncle (who goes by El Maistro) at El Mesquite. When you aren't told why you are invited—yeah right, "invited"—to go to the town of San Ygnacio and meet at the mesquite tree ranch, chances are high you won't make it back. Especially at one in the afternoon.

My tio is the number one drug runner in the South Texas border, and he didn't get to be number one by being nice or understanding. He knows all the angles. He's swift to action, and he's all business. I better add that he's paranoid as shit and a real stone killer. If you met my tio, you wouldn't think much about him. He's six feet with boots on, 180 lbs. He dresses classic South Texas—boots, bland shirt, and a straw cowboy hat. He's not flashy like me, but he has a way of turning a switch that transforms him into one scary cat you do not want to cross.

Growing up, Tio was a small, thin runt that got his clock cleaned on a weekly basis. The story goes, when he was twelve, a kid kept jacking him up, so my tio went into his dad's barn and got a whip. He went looking for this kid at school and whipped him half to death before the principal pulled my tio off. When the principal retired twenty years later, he still had a scar on his left cheek from the confrontation. Nobody ever messed with my tio again; the whole town labeled him crazy.

When he graduated from tenth grade, he made friends with some Mexican dudes that introduced him to the cartel, and he took to that lifestyle like fat to a mother-in-law. My tio had to prove himself to the cartel by taking a machete and hacking up a guy he knew. Job interviews in the cartel are really not what you want to be a part of.

So yeah, my tio and I booze from the same gallery, but we don't sit at the same table. He would kill his best friend, or even his brother; I couldn't do that, and that is enough distinction. People recognize the difference between us, and that makes my tio a bit nervous.

Believe it or not, his second-in-command makes him look like a monja. South Texas only knows this guy as "El Machete," and he earned the name. This guy was brought in from Chapas, Mexico, where I heard he did some things that won't get him any church prizes. His thing was handling snitches, which has always been the main problem for all drug runners. He reminds me of the guy that tortured the cop in *Reservoir Dogs*. You know, the kind of criminal that dances, lathers himself up while he's torching and killing someone, loving every second of it.

The story goes, they caught a guy from Mexico running drugs in my tio's backyard. El Machete took this poor bastard to El Ranchito, dragged him into the barn, and tied him up. The Mexican began spilling everything from where his money was to where the drugs were stashed. All Machete kept saying, in broken English, was: "I'm not here to ask you anything, puto." What he did to this guy after slicking him up is still talked about to this day. El Machete took him, barely alive, to a tree where he tied him up, cut a hole in his stomach, pulled out about four feet of guts, and tied those to a stake. That way, the dude could see what the coyotes were having for dinner. Yeah, at the mesquite meeting, he's the guy to watch. If he reaches in the backseat, as I have seen him do many times, he will kill somebody.

I need some esquina at this meeting. I hope my boys are home, or I'm fucked. Calling Paco and Rigo, my adopted brothers and crew, is my only chance of making it out alive. Having a meeting at El Mesquite Ranch in San Ygnacio at one in the afternoon is about as safe as walking into a deserted barn unarmed and blindfolded to meet Charles Manson. At one, the traffic is nonexistent because it's siesta time for us Texicans.

These guys have been with me on jobs that people thought we would never pull off, or even make it out alive. Together, we actually make up one great crew. My tio knows this, even though he doesn't speak of it.

The phone rings ten times before Rigo answers. Sounds like he's been out all night, too.

"I need you and Paco up and running, right now. I'll be there in thirty. Have Paco break out his .308. Yeah, yeah, I'll explain when I get there, pendejo."

Rigo asks too many questions. Here we go....

"It is serious, Rigo."

More questions....

"Maybe, Rigo. I'm not sure, and that's what's bothering me. See you in thirty."

I hang up with Rigo still mumbling on the other end.

Now I need to get my head straight. I grab both Glocks and the two mags, all loaded up with seventeen rounds apiece. My cold steel fila and berretta .25 cal. are tucked in my boot, and my cover knife is secure on my belt. Everybody, from the cops to the crooks, always takes my belt knife but they usually miss my cold steel knife with the Tanto blade, which is my best weapon. If you have a gun at your waist and I have my knife, you will never clear leather. In South Texas, you better be good with the blade. Everybody has one and knows how to use it.

I head out to my Ford King Ranch P/U, a bull of a truck that runs like a scalded ape—in my world, you are what you drive. As I load it up, I go over all the possible scenarios in my mind. This meet stinks to high heaven. Why the meet, and why did he page at 5:00 a.m.? Nothing makes sense. If my tio wanted to kill me, he wouldn't give me the heads up; he would just wait to catch me in my element, soft kill me with a friend quietly walking up and BOOM!

No, he wants something. But what, I do not know. I'll have to wait and see.

On my way to Zapata, I have to drive over the Veleño Bridge on Falcon Lake. Man, how many good times I've had fishing and swimming. Fish frys, under the bridge. My whole life has been in Zapata, but it hasn't been dull. The things happening in these South Texas towns, nobody would believe. I have seen beatings, stabbings, murders, and rapes go by the wayside because of who you are or who you know. I saw one dude beat a guy with a chair— he beat him half to death and sat back at the bar to finish his beer. The deputies came and the ambulance took him to the hospital. They asked the chair swinger—that happened to be the county judge's brother—to please follow them to the courthouse so the sheriff could PR bond him. He went, filled out the paperwork, and then drove his drunk ass home fifteen minutes later. South Texas at it's finest.

My boys' house is on the east side of town, called the Medina Edition. It isn't the safest part. If you're looking for trouble, Medina is waiting.

Puta madre. Every time I pull up to Rigo and Paco's house, their fucking dogs maul my truck, jumping up and scratching the shit out of it. This truck guzzles more gas-ofa than Rigo drinks beer, but I still don't want their damn dogs ruining the paint job.

"Paco, call you're fucking dogs off or I'll shoot their asses."

Rigo steps out from the side of the house.

"I see you, joto. Don't try to flank me, and I can see Paco on the roof. Why do you guys do this every time? Paco," I yell up, "don't wear your hunting camo on a tin roof. I saw you when I hit the hill behind your house, pendejo."

Paco is a real deep thinker. Don't get me wrong, he has guts. But he's always been too scared to try anything on his own. He's tough as nails, even though he's a tiny moth-erfucker; couldn't reach six feet on his tippy toes and weighing maybe a buck fifty with his boots on. He's got the traditional jet-black Mexican hair, like everyone, except his is curly. And he's got these happy eyes. You can never tell when this guy is going for his pistol. He can be smiling and pumping rounds in your ass at the same time.

Paco has the makings of a great crew boss, but hates to be on the spot for any answers. He hates being ques-tioned—that would mean making a decision, and he would rather kick than think. That is something his dad beat into him years ago. *"You wanna stay alive? Don't make deci-sions."*

His dad told us a story when we were kids. He said he was asking the wisest Mexican in the town—who was 109 years old—the secret to a long life. The old man said the secret to a long life is to mind your own fucking business. Paco and Rigo's dad would then say, *"Mind your business and stay alive."* What a guy. Hey, more than what my padre taught me.

Rigo is the muscle of the crew, bigger and stronger than Paco, with a punch that would kill a donkey. The two of us can handle ourselves, but Rigo feels no pain and has no quit to him, even when he's won. He took so many beatings from his dad that no one can hurt him. I could drop Rigo in the North Pole naked, and he would show up at your pool with a suntan and a pocket full of pesos; that's who he is. But Rigo is also more of a loose cannon and a bit crazy, as you might think. He starts on a scrape with someone, we better be there to pull him off or he will kill the guy. How do you reason with a guy that doesn't feel pain like you or me? You can't.

Rigo runs his mouth all day and asks the stupidest questions at all the wrong times. He once was kicking the shit out of a guy from Laredo over a spilled beer and every time Rigo hit him, he would ask the chump where the dude bought his shirt. He really liked his shirt, I guess.

I try to herd them into my truck, advising them we have a little job to do. Paco, having a little more sense than Rigo, wants to tailgate before we go anywhere. Tailgating is how everything is discussed in South Texas. You go to the back of your truck, put your foot on the bumper, usually with a beer in hand, and you lean on the tailgate and talk it over.

"Your mom's home, right?"

Rigo looks around and says, "En la casa."

"Okay, then let's just talk English and we'll be fine." I once asked their mom why she never learned English. She said: *"It's South Texas. We speak Spanish here."* Of course, she said that in Spanish.

I began to explain to the guys about the page I got.

Rigo interrupts, "Your uncle paged you at five?"

"Yeah, I know, right. But I didn't call him back till 9:30."

Paco gives me the "what the fuck is wrong with you, are you crazy?" look.

Rigo says, "Fuck him. That guy ain't God."

"Around here he is, and it gets worse. He wants me to meet him in San Ygnacio, at El Mesquite at one today."

"Toño, you know everybody is at home eating and taking a siesta. It's busier at 3:00 a.m., vato."

"I know, Rigo. That's why I'm here talking to you guys, my crew. You guys know El Machete will be with him."

"What did you do, ese? You go on your own with some deal?"

"I don't go on my own, and if I did, I wouldn't be here. I'd go alone. And if I had done something, I would know how to size it up. But I got nothing. You guys do anything?"

"No, no, joto, don't put this on us. We are the muscle, you are the brains."

"Hey, I had to ask. Well, we are a crew, so you guys down with this meet?"

"I'll get my .308 for the meet, but you tell me what I'm supposed to do with it, Toño."

"I will. As soon as I come up with something."

"I really like this truck, Toño. Can I have it if you get dropped?"

"No. Vales verga, Rigo, you know I used the money from the last load to buy it."

"Bullshit. You spent the money on putas and virongas."

As the guys are getting their tools ready, my mind drifts back to what my tio could want. It makes no sense.

"Okay, Paco, I'm going to need you to load that deer slayer and do a creep to cover us from a ridge close to El Mesquite. If you can get south, you can get a clear shot. I'll have to drop you short of the meet, and you'll have to haul ass to get set up.

Rigo shrugs. "Dude, maybe he just wants to give us a job?"

"You really want to take that chance? You know what happened to La Chinche, and that was his godson. Shit, he hacked the guy up himself, yelling the whole time, 'Steal from me!' I never knew he had a row of machetes. He uses one for cutting, one for slashing, one for beating, and one for chopping parts off. Each one has a different weight and length. Sick fuck."

We all take a moment, thinking about that event.

"Paco, when you get set up, keep a close eye on that fat fuck Machete. If he reaches in the backseat, snap his head like Kennedy."

"Why you have to go there?"

That comment lit Rigo up. It is said their dad was one of the shooters on the grassy knoll. Supposedly, Woody Harrelson's dad was with him, but that's a different story.

"I have my Glocks. You need one?"

Rigo reaches for his Colt Python revolver.

"Dude, it only has six rounds."

Rigo holds up two fingers. "Two rounds are all I need." He gives that comical look and crazy smirk of his. I am glad he's on my side.

I turn back to Paco. "Remember, my tio knows all the tricks, so he probably figured you two in the mix. That's how he thinks."

"Fuck that guy. We're true Zapata river rats," Rigo says with pride.

The drive from Zapata to San Ygnacio is only fifteen minutes, but today it feels days long. Along Highway 83, the river separates Texas and Mexico. It gets me every time—for those who see past the rocks and thorns, it's majestic territory. It's such a short trip to another world, so different from Texas. Different rules in our line of work, that's for sure. Before we get to San Ygnacio, we can see the top of the entrance to El Mesquite Ranch, a half-mile up—a big old metal gate with a cattle guard you have to drive over. There are no cattle on the ranch, but they keep the guard. It makes a distinct noise, like an alarm for any unwanted visitors.

"Paco, when I make the turn, bail and wachale, bro."

"Slow down and give him time to make the hill. Give him that soft dirt to bail."

I slow 'er down. Paco bails, does a tuck and roll, and he's on the trot.

"Rigo, I'll give Paco time to get set up, but you stay in the truck. Take my Glock. You better double tap everyone if it turns to shit. I don't want to get chopped up, so don't leave me on the dangle."

Rigo nods instead of answering; that's an indicator he's sweating the meeting.

"Orale! Let's do it."

As we drive over the hill, I see my tio's truck and El Machete's Caddy. El Machete drives an '88 Deville because he can fit four bodies in the trunk. The dude even scares me, and I don't shake. El Machete is your typical fat Mexican, but he's got no whiskers on his fat face because he's full Indian of some clan. Mayan, I think. He dresses like a pimp: guayavera shirt with all the pockets, like the old-time barbers used to wear; Sansabelt pants; and Stacy Adam shoes. Not even the whores want anything to do with

him. But his shirts always match his candy apple red
Caddy. At least he's got that. I can't picture El Machete
driving anything else.

Tio is just standing like a statue, leaning on his tailgate. He looks like an old-fashioned Mexican actor, like
Pedro Infante or Augustin Lara.

Mesquite Ranch is far enough from the highway that
nobody can see the happenings. The ranch fits my tio's
character, with a small patio made of oil field pipe ce-
mented in the ground. That way, if they decide to tie you
up, you will not be able to yank your way out and dash.
Tio thinks everything through, to the last detail. I remember the table under the patio; some things, you never can
unsee.

But I can't get that in my mind right now, or it will
show. I have to show strength and confidence, not fear.

2

SAN YGNACIO

I pull up and step out of my truck. There's Tio, still tailgating with El Machete. I walk up. He's staring straight into me with his beady little eyes. They're dark like his heart would be, if he had one.

"Hey, Tio, que onda?"

"Yeah, raise your shirt up and turn around."

I'm on the same team as this guy—this is the world I live in. As I start my turn, I know he's going to spot one of my Glocks in the small of my back. He knows it, too. Why he just doesn't ask if I'm packing, I have no idea. We have to do this same routine every time.

"Leave your gun, knife, on the hood."

"Chingado, Tio, I'm not La Jura."

"Just do it, mijo."

"Okay, I'm clean. You want to tell me what this wato is all about?"

"You telling me what to do?"

"No, Tio, I'm just a bit worried why I'm here and why Machete is flanking me."

"You have a job, you and your two pendejo brothers.

Right there I knew I was going to live to worry another day. He could have said, "You have to kill the pope," and I would've smiled.

"Tio, they might be stupid, but loyal as real brothers."

"Shut up. You do this job, and you guys get to stay alive."

"What the fuck did we do, Tio?"

"You fucked up, mijo. You guys floated the wrong vato in the Valley. That guy you fidiolaste on South Padre Island was the son of my link in Mexico. That guy has people like *me* buried. You fucked up bad, ese, knifing him like that. So now you have to do this job and do it just right to keep me in good graces with him, or I will have to do my end."

...Chingado.

"Mijo, I don't want to do it. You're my guy, but business is business. Don't make me have to do it. You know I will. Don't make me."

I nod like a good soldier. You're not given an option, but you still get the ritualistic question: "Do you want to take the job?" You have to know when to shut up and listen.

"Now, this son of his was a pain in the ass, and it was said he was talking to the narcs, so he isn't as mad as you would think. You do this job right and you and your crew get a pass."

"Chingado, Tio, that guy pulled a knife and tried to cut me. He had it coming."

"We all have it coming—it's just a matter of when. I told him you were levelheaded, and if you did it, then it had to be done. Did you have to do it?"

"He would have killed me. That rich Mexican pulled a turn and poke, but I spotted him walking up with his hand cupped and that 'oh shit' look on his face. He didn't know who he was walking into. But why was he coming at me, Tio? You know?"

"I don't know, mijo. A girl, a look, your fancy boots. He's from Mexico, how the hell can anybody know why they do shit? Not too many, if any, are better with a blade than you—except me, of course. That was his fate. His destiny to die at your fast hands. Now, this is yours."

I remember the night I gutted that turd like it was yesterday. We had made a money drop for my tio in Brownsville to a slick Mexican dude wearing a lime green leisure suit by the border of Reynosa, Mexico. It was Rigo, Paco, and me on the drop, and it went down without a hitch. We told my tio we were going to be partying in South Padre Island and to not expect us for a couple of days. We were clean, no dope or OPM (other people's money), so we were cool for school. We called some running buddies from Edinburg to come down and have a pachanga and check out some of the South Texas girls in beachwear.

We checked into the Island Inn hotel on the strip and broke out a bottle of Pappy Van Winkle whisky we had taken from a guy that owed us some money. We cleaned up and by 9:00 p.m., we were at Louie's Backyard Bar having a large time. The Edinburg boys showed up drunk, of course, yelling, "Edinburg Lancers, con safo!" Yeah, they're very proud of their high school team, I guess, even though they're fucking forty now.

We were all on the outside patio when I noticed a dark-skinned Mexican—not a Texican—glaring at me from inside the bar. Now, I know we were loud and pissing the locals off, so I didn't think twice about this twenty-year-old border jumper. I did notice he was wearing Wrangler dress pants, a long-sleeved cowboy shirt, and silver tips on his pointy, black boots. Those were something; they didn't work with the rest of his low-end, blue-collar attire at all. I'm not knocking affordable clothing, but the tips? That was odd, and I did make note of that, but chalked it up to bad taste—another Mexican standing out in a crowd of Hawaiian shirts and Bermuda shorts. Wouldn't be the first time. I walked over to the edge of the outside bar to order another round of beers, and that's when I felt this cold chill, and time just stopped.

I glanced to my rear and I saw the shitty-dressed Mexican on what we call "the quick walk"—before you do an action (a hit). He was almost on me. His right hand was cupped, so I knew it was a blade, not a pistol. I spun to my left, flicking my cold steel open and "punched" him between his upper left ribs three times. I caught him in my arms.

Turning, smiling at the bartender, I said, "He is drunk, bro."

I carried him down the stairs and dropped him in the ocean very quietly. I'm just glad he didn't try it in the middle of the bar. We would have let him drop and calmly walked out of the bar, but we would have been made by somebody.

"Okay, agree that you do the job?"

"Yes, Tio. Consider it done, whatever it is."

"You still have friends in Nuevo Laredo?"

"Aw, fuck. It's across?" I hate doing work in Nuevo Laredo.

Tio gives me that look that asks for no words, just demands submission.

"Sorry, Tio, I know you hate whining. What is it?"

As my tio lays it out, I start getting a cold chill in 100-plus-degree heat. I get the feeling of being tossed in the Rio

Grande wearing cement blocks on my feet—just like El Toro, but that's another story altogether.

"Now get out of here and go do the job. And it better be done fast, like two days."

"Two days?"

My tio stares at me like I just kicked his dog. You don't kick a man's dog in South Texas; that gets you dead.

As I turn and walk back to the truck, Tio shouts, "Oh, and Mijo, next time leave Paco in the truck. I don't want to kill him just to show you what's who, okay?"

Shit, Tio, I have to do what I was taught and remember who taught me. "I know."

"Next time, he stays in the truck, or get your minds around being a floating fish buffet."

That fat Machete starts his fucked up laugh, but in a fucked up way, like he's going to enjoy whatever game this is. He never liked me from the get-go. I bet he would love to get me in the shed with his toys. He's too stupid to hide any tells. I get a really bad feeling about this piece of work we are about to twist off.

As I start walking back to my truck, I sense an air of betrayal hovering over my head. Rigo is sitting in the cab with this bewildered look on his face, a thing of beauty. As soon as I hop in, it starts.

"Toño, that pinche puto jerkoff scares the shit out of me."

"Fuck it. Let's go get Paco."

"Toño, there he is in the brush by the road. Look at him! He thinks he's Joe sniper." Rigo flashes his patented shit-eating grin. "Don't stop, just slow down just enough. Paco, get your ass in. You were made, apurate."

"Yeah, he knew you were covering us. He said next time stay in the truck."

"Shit, I thought I caught a glimmer of glass to my east, but the sun was in my eyes. That was a Houdini move. I got to remember that one."

"Well, if the sun was in your eyes then the other shooter wanted you to spot him...that does not add up."

"Well, Toño, what was so important that we had to shit our pants?" Rigo asks as Paco settles in.

"Let me drop you guys off at your chante. Give me a couple hours to think and get some things in order. I'll have it worked out in my head by then."

Rigo wants to press me; it's in his nature. He keeps a lid on it, but I can tell cause his damn foot is tapping and it's making his knee jitter. They are as loyal as my Rott-weilers, these two homeboys.

As I am driving back to Zapata, Rigo and Paco are bitching back and forth nonstop. Fighting brings them comfort and keeps them calm. *How could Paco have been so stupid...? Why does Rigo only have a six-shooter...?* Listening to this goes back to junior high, when they used to fight about girls, horses, and trucks. All I had to say back then to start the argument was, "I really think the Ford trucks are better than the Ram," and it was on like Donkey Kong. It's fun until somebody else jumps in to the argument. Never get between these brothers, because it will be the death of you.

I pull up to their house. Shit, the ride back was longer than the ride there. "Get out!" I bark. "Be back in a couple."

This spin with my tio is hard enough to figure out without these whistle britches clamoring in my ear. They hop out and pick at each other all the way in. I swear, it's like two old ladies after church.

This is the part I hate to roll out to the guys, because it's a job that has no good ending I can think of. I have to conjure a plan to save our asses. Going to Nuevo Laredo to do a piece of work is the hardest thing I can imagine. It is a world of drugs, killing, and mistrust at every turn. It's as dangerous as going to an LA Raiders game. You can't find anyone to pay off that wouldn't turn you in for a second payoff.

We did a piece of work two years ago on the Nuevo Laredo border, and we were lucky to get out with our skin. All we had to do was pick up a package for my tio and deliver it to a guy in Eagle Pass, Texas. The package was in a locked ice chest. I figured I would only need one guy, so I took Rigo for the muscle, just in case. We picked the package up at the Cadillac Bar in Nuevo Laredo from a horse trainer. He explained the ice chest had horse semen from some famous racehorse. It was worth a lot of money, and we had a timeframe of six hours before it would be worthless.

We thought it was a cakewalk but turned into a shitstorm. We had federales pulling up in vehicles, so Rigo grabbed the ice chest, ran to the kitchen, placed it in a freezer. I walked behind the bar, where Don Ramon—the bartender for the last fifty years and famous for his Slow Gin Fizz—threw me a white coat and made me an honorary bartender. Rigo stayed in the kitchen, washing dishes. The horse trainer was on his own and just sat there with that not-so-smart look on his face.

...Seconds pass and the federales blow in and grab the guy, dumb face and all. They press him to tell them where the horse cum is. They take him outside and do the Nuevo Laredo cop trick. The roads are rock and gravel, so when they knock you to the ground, they say, "So you trying to pick up rocks?" and begin to wear you out.

Rigo sticks his head out from the kitchen and I toss my coat to Don Ramon with a "thank you," and we bolt out the back with the horse gizz in the ice chest. We walk to the bridge and cross back into Laredo. We actually crossed the bridge with horse daddy juice, and the immigration officer doesn't even ask what's in the chest. We jump in our truck, haul ass to Eagle Pass, and deliver the horse batter to our contact. Can you imagine going to jail in Nuevo Laredo, Mexico for trafficking horse love juice? Embarrassing.

And here I am going back there.

Damn, what the hell have I got myself into? And what's my tio's angle? He should have killed me on the spot if his main Mexican source was in jeopardy. He said the Mexican I dropped was a pain in the ass, but blood is blood. That's picking at my brain like a crow on a dead cow. I have to find the angle, a plan to get us out of this grinder.

Who was that Mexican I dropped in South Padre? What was he doing before he got himself killed? Maybe that's the missing link here. Or, what does he have to do with this job? Why is this coming up six months after I dropped him? Who exactly is his dad? I need to reach out to some compadres to get me the skinny on this situation. I can't use my family in the Valley, because word will get back to my tio, and that would be like a turd in the punchbowl, to say the least.

I can make some calls to the middle civilians—they owe me—and maybe get some answers to all this mess. Middle civilians are like the floor tile workers in building a house. They don't make the deals or put up any money, but without them, you can't walk into the house. The job itself is simple: drive to Nuevo Laredo, snatch a ruka, bring her back gift-wrapped (meaning alive) to my tio at El Mesquite. According to El Quate, a reliable contact and good friend of the family, the ruka is a girlfriend of a high-ranking guy in the Federales. She's at a secure compound with ten or so men—well-armed soldiers from the Mexican Army. Easy my ass. The thought of crossing that bridge into Mexico from Laredo is a trap in itself. Everybody will know we are in town within thirty minutes of us crossing, and they'll want to take us for whatever we have.

The other problem is our weapons and ammo. We have to get that across and back without getting thrown in "La Loma," Nuevo Laredo jail. Can you imagine how bad you have to be to get tossed in a Mexican jail? The jail is on a hill, hence the name La Loma. It is made to keep you in, not to keep you safe inside. The guards are all paid for, so if you're a new fish, you better have money or property they can use or sell, or they could kill you after they use you up, if you know what I mean. If you want to eat while visiting La Loma, you have to have your food brought in by family or friends. It's not Club Fed!

And then, there's getting the ruka back across the border. Simple my ass.

First things first—I have to hire a guide to maneuver us around Nuevo Laredo. I have just the villain in mind. Jay is a guy who's been a reliable friend, but he's as crazy as a shithouse rat. I just hope he isn't on the lamb for some other job. This guy is from the streets of Laredo. At a young age, Jay got hooked up with the Tejas Riatas—one of the most ruthless gangs on the border. They've done everything from drug trafficking to kidnapping. And hits—they're responsible for more successful hits at the border and the Mexico interior than Pancho Villa and his merry men. But they never did the hard hits in Texas; this is why they've done so well.

Jay was the hardest of the pack and captain of the most ruthless crew in the Riatas gang. He was smart and loyal to a fault. They knew he could do the time, so they sacrificed him more than once, and that broke him. Then to add to it, he got old and drank too much, so they put him out to pasture. You might not believe this, but it's not like TV; they do have retirement in the gangs and treat the vets with respect and honor. They don't exactly have a 401K, and they sure as fuck don't collect Social Security, so Jay freelances for people like my tio—and for me when a job comes up that's slippery and needs a true craftsman. I hope he's around to get us the info on the girl's movements and to secure transportation—get us in and out of Nuevo without getting our balls chopped off.

Before I go pick up the guys to fill them in on this death march, I got to grab supplies. Buying ammo is a red flag in Zapata. I'll have to go to the Western Auto and buy my shit. I know I'll be grilled about what I'm up to. Shit, my guts are stinging, just like when you shoot Mescal that's been laying on the backseat of your truck with 100-degree heat beating down on it through the window.

As I walk into the store, "El Red," Julian Moto, eyes me from behind the counter. I was ready for it; the guy's been eyeing me for years. El Red is several years older than me.

We grew up playing basketball since I could walk. This guy had a thrity-point game average in high school. He could have played pro ball, but a case of the stupids, along with case after case of beer, ended that before it began. He's one bigass Mexican, and he's all muscle, too. As I walk up to the counter, I can already tell this is going to be a bitch.

"Hey, Red, I need hunting ammo and beer can bullets for the ranch."

"Que paso, Sep."

Sep's a nickname from way back. It's short for brush. I had a flat top as a kid—you know, like a brush. Red was the only guy I could not beat in a one-on-one basketball game, and he will never let me forget it. Calling me Sep is one of his reminders—my nickname during games.

"So, what are you really up to, buying all this ammo?"

"Red, stay out of it. It's just for fun, man."

He gives me that glare. He is the only guy that can read my body language because of all the years of playing ball with him. You can learn a lot about a person from that.

"Don't try that spin move with me. I know you."

"Red, if you do—you know not to ask. Just bring up the .308 cal. and 9mm half case, and let it go."

"Puto, don't talk to me like that. I'll kick your ass."

"Just do it and let it go, or I'll tell your grandmother what you did with her car last week."

"Okay." Red pulls on both sides of his bigass mustache and cracks a smirk. "Leave my grandmother out of it. I'll get your shit."

It's always nice to have lived with people all your life, because you know all their secrets. "Put it on my account, and keep your mouth shut, because I'll find out and you don't want it to go there."

"Sep, we're playing at the Lions Club tomorrow. You gonna be there?"

"Not tomorrow. I'll try to catch up next week."

As I start to pick up the ammo, Red grabs my arm. When Red grabs your arm, you're not going anywhere.

He looks at me intensely. "You need any help?"

"Naw, Red, I got it. Not a big thing. I'll see you on the court, my friend."

Red lets go and nods a goodbye.

"Red, I'll see you again and I'll bring the beer." I turn and walk away, but I can't seem to shake that he can read the trouble in me. Red is a good friend, but a civilian, and he doesn't need to get mixed up in river rat drug running— or the body-snatching business. I haul ass to my chante to shower again and change my clothes.

My most difficult task at this place and time is figuring out what I am going to wear for this fiasco. It could be my last opportunity to wear my cool duds. If I am going out, I'm going out in style. I'm busting out my Skully retro black shirt with white piping—the one with skulls embroidered on the front. My Affliction jeans with crosses embroidered down my left leg with just a bit of flair on the bottom. Boots-wise, I am going with my Bed and Stu lace-ups. They're distressed and comfortable for the dash. I never wear them around town, because they are just to cool for these nimrods. Yeah, a last stand ensemble. Just like Travis and Bowie, except I would have been next to Santa Anna.

Pulling into my driveway, a hundred yards out, I hear my dogs barking. I have to feed the mutts and call my maid to feed them until I return. I also have to write a letter for her, just in case I don't make it back. I have written several of these letters to my maid and every time, she gives me the same advice: *"Mijo, please stop what you're doing. It's killing your mother."* My maid and her family have worked for us since they crossed the river looking for a better life. I wish I could explain the situation to her, but it would fall on deaf ears. Some people never look up to see what is happening around them. It's easier to look at the ground and hope for a good outcome. I can't blame her. It is much easier than having to squint your eyes at the truth.

Hell, it's only money and stuff. My mama keeps all my feria and my house is in her name. I don't mind dying, but I'd want to die for a reason—not because my tio says so. Not this time. I'm going to fuck that guy, one way or another. I'm going to fuck his world up right.

Driving to Rigo and Paco's house, I'm coming up with a stunt we pulled years ago when we grabbed a dude from Freer, Texas. It was a slick snatch, and he paid my tio his money, so he made it out alive. It cost him a finger and three broken toes, but that's another story. This trick can work, but it has to have great timing and a lot of luck. Jay will have to get info for us on the ruka's movements. We need a diversion, and a boat to cross the Rio Grande. Simple, right? Shit, as soon as we ask about the ruka or order a boat from this river rat, the whole town will know we are up to something. Also, I hope this one goes a little smoother. I don't want the ruka to lose any fingers. Women look better with all their fingers.

I can't get the dead Mexican out of my mind. What does he really have to do with this snatch and grab? Why six months later? And who is this dad that hasn't dropped us? And why? I made some calls to the outskirts of the family and they're trying to find out about these guys for me. This isn't right, not in any way, shape, or form.

As I pull up to my crew's house, I'm sweating already. I have to give them a plan they can buy and execute. It's like anything else—you have to have buy in, or it won't work. Rigo is outside waiting, and you can tell he's uneasy by the way he's moving—he's rocking and rocking like a baby in his mom's arms.

"Rigo, I got the ammo. Where's Paco?"

"Inside. Oiling the barrel and getting the case cover ready to wrap the rifle, in case we need to get wet."

Shit, I didn't think of illegally crossing, but we don't have the time to get a ride to the city from the river. "No, he won't need to plastic it up. We're going across the bridge into Nuevo Laredo. And wait—did you just guess we were going to the Nuevo Laredo?"

"Toño, we're getting ready for anything. Are you kidding me, with all the ammo and guns? I hate going to Nuevo. You know I was tossed in La Loma. I was in last year for two hours before Paco got me out, and it was like being in Hell for an eternity."

"Listen, we will get into Nuevo with all our hardware, and we will get out alive."

"How the hell are we gonna do that? You have a guard at the bridge, don't you?"

"Not yet, but we will by the time we roll up. Get Paco. Let's go through the plan."

Waiting for Paco, I'm still getting the plan worked out in my mind. Every piece is harder than the next, but it can be done. It has to work, or we die in Mexico, where there are no funerals or churches—just a hole we get dropped in. That's the life we had to take because of where we grew up and the choices we didn't have. These guys own us because we have families that chain us to the world of drug running and all that goes with it. Choices are not in the mix. "You don't want to work for me?" they say. Your family disappears in a ranch. It's just that simple. After a while, it is what you are.

"Rigo, load your stuff in the back and let's drive up to the hill outside of town. I'll lay out the plan."

"Toño, I don't know...."

"I know, but you make it sound like we have a choice, brother."

"I know, but you can't tell me all this wato is over a Mexican puto you floated. It can't be all about him."

"You're right. There's more to it. Too much time has passed, but I haven't found out what's the real deal and why this ruka is so important to my tio. But I'm working on it."

"I have a bad feeling about this one, loco."

"You always have bad feeling about the job. That's what helps me get through the day."

3

TAILGATING

As we drive up to the scenic park we call "the hill outside of town," we're stiff and on edge like whores in church. I stop on the hill and look around for snowbirds—they frequent the hill so they don't have to pay a lousy thirty bucks in a RV park.

"It's all clear, Toño," Rigo announces, like he's the only one with eyes. "It's nut-cutting time. What the fuck are we going to do?"

Rigo doesn't even bother to get into tailgate stance before he starts in. He's such a nervous, chatty bastard.

"Before you say anything else, we aren't going to pull a 'turn and go' and kill my tio—which I did think about."

"I was just about to say that, burn him down and that fat fuck Machete, too."

"Yeah, but who are their employers?"

"Yeah, I know it can't happen without our families getting cut into pieces. They would make an example."

"If we did that, they would have to. But I'm working on it. The job is to go to Nuevo Laredo, snatch a girl, and bring her back to El Mesquite unharmed in two days. Shut up, Rigo. Before you say another word, shut up and let me lay it out first, then motherfuck me."

Rigo works hard to keep a lid on it. He actually starts sweating, and it ain't from the sun.

"Okay, this is what I got worked out so far. I think if we do it just right, and we have a lot of luck, we can get to Nuevo, grab the girl, and be back to Zapata. After that, I have to figure out how important this ruka is, and how we can use her as a stay-alive chip."

They both seem to be with me so far.

"First, we need to have a guide in Nuevo that is trustworthy and knows the guards at the border bridge."

"Who the hell has that contact and wouldn't flip us for a reward?"

And I've lost them.

"Wait, are you thinking about that crazy pachuco, Jay? Dude, he is a true psycho. And he hates Paco."

"Actually, he hates you, Rigo."

Rigo knows this. Why he'd pin it on Paco? Probably just trying to start a fight to distract his sweat glands, which are working overtime right now. Paco doesn't even flinch; he just smiles with those goddamn eyes like he doesn't have a care in the world, like someone just handed him a cold beer. Sometimes, I think Paco's smarter than every damn one of us. When God handed out the big brains, Paco was first in line. Hell, most of the time, I wish I was Paco. He has great ideas, but whispers in my ear so I can put them out to the boss. Most people in my world see problems at eye level. Paco seems to view problems from a different position. I always think he's standing on a windmill, looking at the problem from a completely different angle. Yeah, Paco is the still water in a running river. Having him as my right-hand man has kept me alive this long. I hope he never knows it, or I might be in my tio's shoes someday. Right now, Paco and Rigo help me sleep better at night—well, more like pass out, but you get the drift.

Rigo says, "You have anybody else that won't cave and won't backstab us?"

"Jay wouldn't do that. He has a thing about honor and keeping his word."

"Toño, he's crazy. Loco like a three-legged dog."

"Crazy is what we will need on this gig, and he has brass balls. He never backs down or quits until the job is done. He also has a guy that knows a guy with info on the girl's movements, and he's got a guy that runs dope across the river with a boat. We need that boat to get this done right and done fast. All I have to do is convince him to do the job. So, Rigo, keep your mouth shut and don't piss him off like last time."

"Dude, all I asked him was about his tats."

"Right, so don't ask him about his tats. He's very sensitive about them, all fifty of 'em. We have to get him to get us a diversion, a car for the snatch and grab. Jay's a big part of us staying alive, so play nice. Why do you have be such a fucking downer, Rigo? Be more like Paco. Goddamn optimist over here, nodding and swaying and not saying shit."

I give Paco a hearty slap on the shoulder. He nods an atta boy.

"So that's it, boys—we cross the bridge using one of Jay's friends on the border, get intel on where the girl is, snatch her, and boat across to Texas."

Easy.

Finally, Paco speaks. "Toño, do you even know who this ruka is? What she looks like? And who is coming to get her once we grab her?"

"She's the Federal Commandante's girlfriend, or slave or something. El Quate, our oracle in Zapata, gave me the skinny on her. She's bien wenona, black hair, green eyes, and a body worth killing over. She's from Colombia or someplace like that. Around twenty-five years old, he thinks. She must be a pro or well trained to have him keep her around.

"Who is El Commandante, Toño?"

"Who is El Commandante? You've heard of Contreras. Rigo. No mames. He's the same fuck that had all the heads cut off his competition, and then put them in a circle in the middle of the plaza."

"Oh, him. Not that guy, please not that guy. He is a devil straight from hell, living in a fucking castle in the middle of Mexico. That guy is worse than your tio and all his Mexican crew put together, and that monster has an army behind him. Why does your tio want that girl? What does the Mexican have to do with this?"

"I don't know, but we better find out before we drop her off."

"Who do you have working on that?"

"El Quate and the outskirts from the Valley. They owe me big from the thing we did for them in Brownsville last time."

"What makes you think they won't tell your tio?"

"They gave me their word, and that's what they live by. You know that."

You remember when the valley guys called us about how our tractor trailer was going to get hi-jacked by the Morelo boys. They could have easily said nothing. You know why they called? They owed us, for no other reason.

They put themselves in a bad spot just to pay a debt. Yeah, we can trust them."

"I'm just asking questions, Toño. You know how I am."

"Rigo, it's a there-and-back in two days. If you keeping asking questions, we won't get our asses off the back of this truck for another two days."

I'm not asking my crew to pull an action; why do they always have so many questions? I should be stricter with them, but it's too late to be like my tio. I run my crew with respect, and I would not ask them to do anything I wouldn't do.

"El Commandante runs the show in Nuevo and doesn't even keep bodyguards on the ruka, so that's in our favor. She must know something, or has family in Colombia that will do things to get her back, maybe ransom or loads. Either way, she's our key to all this, and she needs to tell us why she is so fucking important to the deal. Without Jay, we have to go in blind and wing the whole job, and that ain't good. So, Rigo, you in?"

"Yeah, I'm in, of course I'm in." He pauses and shrugs. "I guess I'm in."

"What about you, Paco? You guess you're in, too?"

As soon as Paco opens his mouth for a "yes," Rigo chimes in on cue like a church bell at noon on Sunday. "Toño, we are in brother, but know this might be the last time in our hometown. This whole thing sucks, and I hate your tio for doing this to us. Still don't know why we can't hit the old fool—"

"Orale, have some faith, bros. It's just another day on the border."

We wrap up the tailgate and pile in the truck.

Laredo is forty-five minutes from Zapata. With cops everywhere looking for drug runners, we keep to the speed limit and sweat bullets the entire way.

As we pull into Laredo, we get to the first barrio, called Los Mirones. It's called this because any car that drives by, they all come and look out their windows to see who it is and what you're doing in their barrio. We cross into the Three Points barrio—it's known for gambling and where you go to sell stolen shit. You can sell anything there. They also have the best restaurant in Laredo. The Tumble Inn makes the best open BBQ sandwich and serves it with cold-ass beer. I wish we had the time for a refino and virongas, but not today.

We then drive into the worst barrio in town, or possibly the world—El Sal Si Puedes. ("Leave if you can.") This barrio houses the craftiest villains in Texas. You have to have a pair just to drive into this territory. People have said it's like a warzone; not even the cops venture in. They bring out the dead to the cops with the same story: "He just died." Never mind the bullet holes or knife slashes. "Unsolved crime" is what the cops write up, and let the locals work it out.

Damn, the houses are falling apart. It looks like they're rotting—old shotgun houses with leftover cars and fridges used as gates to keep out the wandering thieves. Outside the homes, they have 50K trucks and 100K cars parked by the street so everyone can take a gander and know who is the shit in the barrio. You have to love the drug trade. Texicans can't hide their drug runner status because of the cars they drive. It tells everyone in the barrio who is who and who not to fuck with. These are MexiCANS, not MexiCANTS, if you catch my drift. You can't argue or try to talk your way out of the inevitable outcome. This world isn't like the American Dream, with all its options and understanding. This world is what it is—hard, ruthless, but with great food. If you are in this world and you stray from the path, it will not suffer fools. If this is not understood, they treat you like a snake—cut its head off and skin it.

EL PACHUCO

"Okay, we are coming up to Jay's chante, Rigo. You be cool and don't fuck with him."

"Dude, I got it—no fucking with crazy Jay. I got it."

"I'm going to pull up across the street and let him see us first. He looks to be there. His Dodge purple people eater is parked up like a guard gate."

"Damn, Toño, he does have a sweet ride. 1970 Dodge Road Runner with a 440 engine. I dare you to go up and sit on the hood."

"Man, are you fucking crazy, Rigo? He'll shoot me just on principle. He loves that car more than his eight kids and five wives. Just sit tight. I'm rolling all the windows down so he can see all of us."

As I sit here in the middle of the warzone, I can't believe we are mixed up in this bullshit over a Mexican dude. Or are we just being used for some other reason?

"Wachale! The curtain is moving. If you see a barrel, get ready to haul ass." As I wave out my window, I get this sinking feeling in my gut. What will we do if Jay says no? Or will he just try to collect a bounty on our job? Or just kill us for trying to get him involved in the gig?

Roll the dice.

There he is. Look at this guy in his Stacy Adams shoes, polyester pants, wife beater, and short-sleeve dress shirt— a true pachuco that never made the move to low rider or cholo. Pachucos were before any of them. The dress and language has never changed for these guys. He waves me up to his fence.

"You guys hang here. Let's see where his mind is with all this."

I get out of the truck and start walking toward Jay. As I creep closer, I can see Jay studying my every move. A pachuco always looks for an edge, always wondering if today is the day they get dropped for something or someone in their past. And trust me, there is a lot for Jay to be worried about.

"Jay, que paso, mi pachuco?"

"What do you want, Toño? I'm watching novelas."

"I got a job across that I need your help and your con-
tacts." Damn, jump right into it.

"How much? And do I need to drop anybody?"

"No, bro, it's not an action. Just a piece of work that
my tio needs done. Twenty grand from my pocket, so you
don't have to wait for the sale or transport like usual. I
have it, and it's yours if you do the job."

"Twenty grand from your pocket? What the fuck did
you do now, puto?"

"Brother, you have it right—there is a hole somewhere
in a ranch, waiting for me if this doesn't get done. So that's
why I'm digging in my pocket."

"Toño, I knew your tio before he was the big noise in
the Valley, and I don't trust him for what he has done and
to who."

"I know. But I have no out on this one, and I'm going
to do this, with or without you."

Jay reaches in his back pocket and starts rolling a cig-
arette from a pouch. You know a guy has been in the slam-
mer when he rolls his own. He's been doing that since his
first stretch back in the early seventies.

"How do I know if you get done I'm gonna get paid?"

"I have El Quate holding it for you, and you know he's
a straight-up guy. Even when the feds had him, he never
broke or gave up anything. He did his stretch longer than
most because of it."

44

"I know you and him did some things and you trust him. I trust nobody, ese, but him I respect."

As I unfold the plan, I can see his eyes growing dull and tired by the second.

"You want to do what to who, *and* get back across un-detected and unsuspected? Dude, you have big balls to even think of doing this job, loco. You know they're going to kill your ass as soon as you bring the girl."

"Yeah, I have that to work out. But I'm in a corner, and the room is shrinking around us."

"Us? Who's us? Who's with you on this hunt?"

"Paco and Rigo. I need a crew for this."

Jay throws back his head like a pachuco does when he's about to jump. "Those two putos? They don't have the balls to pull off this type of job."

"We've done some things together. And don't forget the young Bass brother—when he had you in the trunk of the car. I saved your ass that day."

"Why you have to bring that time up, vato. You telling me I owe you for that shit?"

"Jay, he was taking you to the river. The river, ese. Where people don't come back. I took him out with a crow-bar, and thank God he didn't see who did it and I got you out alive, chuco."

The silence between us was thick. The stare from Jay was hard, like tombstones dropping on top of me. A pachuco always pays the debt owed, and Jay was a true pachuco to the bone.

"Mira. Toño—I do this and we are even. Don't ever bring it up again, or I'll kill you. I mean it. Never bring it up. Ever."

I hated to bring it up this time, but I had no choice. It's not like me, and Jay knows that. He knows I wouldn't if I had any other out.

"Ta bien. Let me make some calls and I'll be out later. Just wait with those two pendejos."

"Orale. We will be waiting in the truck. I hope your guy is on the bridge, or this ends before it begins."

As I walk back to the truck, I start feeling like a soulless prick putting these guys in the grinder, all for a pinche Mexican that I floated. It just can't be for that. There has to be more to this. As I look at the guys in the truck, I hope I am not dragging them into a deep hole. They are my family, and I feel like the bad brother holding the shovel. Man, I have to stay frosty and keep my head on straight to work us out of this.

"Okay, Jay is in. He'll be out after he makes some calls to his compass on the bridge and the boat guy. He's also is going to get us a car to cross in. It has compartments for our guns and ammo."

"Toño, that guy is calling your tio right now, flipping on us."

I shake my head at Rigo. "This guy owes me, and I reminded him."

"You brought up a favor to that guy?" Paco says. "Lucky he didn't just shoot you for that. You don't do that to a guy like Jay."

"What am I going to do? He's our only shot at getting it done, or we're dead. We can't run right now, or our families are going to pay for us. We can't do that."

The silence told me I was right. We got our minds onto the job at hand.

As we sit and wait for Jay in the hot Laredo heat, we are quiet, solemn. I don't need to hear Rigo, or anyone else, flapping at the mouth to know everyone is thinking about families and friends right now. Consumed with worry— this is how it works. Every job brings with it the same process. Worry settles in just after the verbal agreements and just before the plan launches into action—every damn time. I turn back to say something, to calm my bros, and see both of them are dead asleep. Fuckers. What do I know? One more minutes passes where I get to further develop my ulcer and listen to those pendajos do the heavy breathing of deep sleep—apparently their consciences are at peace. Good for them.

Jay reappears.

"Okay, here he comes. Wake up and look alive."

Rigo pops his eyes open. "Dude, I swear he looks just like Danny Trejo but taller."

"Rigo, don't start with this guy. He's the real deal, so leave it alone."

"Shit man, look at the way he walks—like he's going to fall backwards with each step."

I turn to Paco. "Talk to him, please."

"Rigo, drop it."

"Esta bien, but just look at him. Remember that movie *Heat,* with Dinero?"

"That's Robert Deniro, pendejo. With an 'e.'"

"Dinero, Deniro, whatever, you know the guy. Anyway, Danny Trejo came out in that movie and the way he dressed and spoke with that vato slang is just like Jay. I bet he helped Trejo in that movie."

"Paco, can you calm your brother down? How could Jay help in a movie in Califas when Jay has never been past Cotulla?"

To tell the truth, Jay is a throwback. Hair all slicked back, wearing cheap Ray-Ban knockoffs. His shoes are pointy and have extra soles on the front—a trademark for pachucos.

"Okay, Paco, move to the back. We need Jay riding shotgun."

"Why the hell do I have to go to the back seat?"

"I need Jay riding front right, Paco. You know he is on point to get us the car with the hide outs and he is our guy to get us across the bridge."

"I'll go back, but I don't like being demoted by a pachuco."

Leave it to Paco to argue about a fucking seat with this job we have to get done. Jay's ass is practically in the front seat by the time he gets around to moving. It's like they're dancing. This pisses Jay off; I can see it. Jay turns around and stares at both the brothers in the backseat. He gives a scoff of displeasure and turns around, flicking his slick black hair back. He keeps his cool, though—werewolf in London. That's what a guy does who's a lifer, a veteran. Someday, if Paco lives a long life, he might be as cool and tough as Jay. I hope.

"Load up, Jay. What's in the bag, homes?"

"I have two grenades for diversions."

Paco and Rigo's eyes look like they're going to pop out. "Shit, where you going to put them? Not back here with us, Jay."

"I'm going to stick them in my pants to keep my pelotas warm, puto. Okay!"

Jay shoves those grenades right down his pants and laughs. "Damn, they are cold!"

"The grenades or your balls, Jay?" Rigo laughs out loud.

"You want me to shove one of these up your ass?"

"A grenade or one of your balls?"

"Dude, Rigo, come on man."

"Okay, Toño. Sorry, Jay, just kidding."

"Yeah, just kidding. Don't fuck with me, Rigo. Tell him, Toño!"

"Okay, Jay. Any luck on your compass?"

"I don't know if I want to talk in front of these pinsoyates."

"This is the crew. So did you get what we needed?"

Jay ignores me. He turns and stares at Rigo and Paco again. It's like tombstones raining down all over again. Paco still has those happy fucking eyes, and Rigo has this smirk on his face. I swear if he said a word, Jay would shove a grenade down his throat. But that's the thing— Paco won't say a damn word. Rigo? I can sense he's really trying to shut up. People think I should have picked a better crew, but they deliver every time.

"What are you looking at, Rigo?"

"Nothing, bro. Just that you looked like Danny Trejo when you were walking up."

That should do it. Jay's going to bail, or kill him, or worse, pull a pin and kill us all. I'm bracing myself. You couldn't hear a razor blade drop, it's so still in here.

"Really? I like that, pachuco," Jay responds. "I've seen all his movies, and he's the shit." Then he smiles like he's on *Candid Camera* and sits back, holding onto half that grin.

"Really, you do look like him."

As Jay continues gloating, I want to turn around and slap Rigo just because, but where would I be? "Jay, anything?"

"Si. My guy is working the bridge until ten tonight, so we have nine hours to cross. Getting in looks a go, but leaving Nuevo with the chick is a different story."

"You get a hold of the guy that knows the ruka's movements around town?"

"Yeah, he's going to meet us at the Montezuma Bar today."

"Montezuma Bar? That's a slaughterhouse. We'll never make it out alive."

Chingado. We are screwed. Paco has it right—it is a slaughterhouse. None of us want to enter.

Jay says, "Hey, that's where I go party all the time."

I have to add, "That should tell you something."

The Montezuma Bar is known as the hangout for all the killers and drug runners in Nuevo Laredo. You don't go there without being known, or without backup—ever. It's even worse than La Perla area in Puerto Rico.

La Perla is a barrio in Puerto Rico where I had to go drop off a load for my tio's connections years back. I had to fly into Miami and meet some guys at the Biltmore Hotel in Coral Gables. This is a nice hotel with a badass pool. Meeting strange Cubans is not my idea of fun. Yeah, I saw *Scarface* and the *Cocaine Cowboys*. A seventy-year-old man and woman knocked on my door and ask for Toño. I swear they looked like retired schoolteachers. I said, "It's me," and they handed me a large suitcase and walked away. I went downstairs, and a nice escalade pulled up and four Cubans asked me to get in. They drove me to Coconut Grove and put me on an Azimut yacht, and off we went to Puerto Rico. These guys set me up with drinks and food, but no girls. I asked them, "Where are the girls?" They stammered in fast Spanish, and all they said about the subject was, "They talk."

Anyway, we land several days later in Viejo, San Juan. They walk me to a Mercedes S500, and I'm a bit nervous. Why they didn't just take the suitcase and move on is still a mystery to me. We drive downtown and pull up to El Morro, where the soldiers used to repel invaders and a wall that circles San Juan's ocean side. La Perla is in the middle of this tourist town, down by the water where nobody ventures. We drive to a house by the water and all I can smell is fish. I'm walked out to a dock where four Boricua natives are cleaning fish and throwing the guts over the edge. A man in a suit is standing at the end of the pier. This guy looks like Ricardo Montalban in a John Philips suit. They point me to him.

As I walk out to this smelly, stinking, ugly pier, he turns around and all he says is "Drop the bag." I was not told to bring anything back, so I drop the bag and say goodbye. This guy raises his hand and I am sure I am going to get hit in this shit pier in shitty Puerto Rico. He asks if I've seen a cockfight. I stammer in my best Spanish, "I'm from South Texas, my friend." We have the best roosters that spur in the world. This guy stares at me, and, like a wave, his mouth breaks into a smile. He then hugs me. "Let me show you my rooster and see what you think." We walk off with the bag still on the pier and he takes me to his fighting rooster training camp up in Los Ramones, by Senderos, where all the rich folk live like Oscar De La Hoya. We had drinks till two in the morning. I was on the plane back to the real world the next day.

This life is a trip.

"Jay, where is the car we are going to cross in?"

"It's at El Indio's, a bar across from Martin High School's parking lot. It has all the compartments for the quetes and tiros."

"How about your boat guy?"

"Yeah, he said all we have to do is tell him where to meet, and he'll bring his seventeen-foot bass tracker boat.

"We also need a guy to wreck his car as a distraction so we can make the grab."

"Fuck that. It's Nuevo Laredo—people get snatched every day. You don't need that."

"We want to snatch her without anybody being wise and calling up El Commandante and his soldiers."

"Okay, I know a guy. But it will cost you."

"We need him to pull it off undetected, Jay."

"Toño, these ideas you have sound really hard to get done. Why don't we just sneak in at night and do the snatch?"

"Guys, that would be great if she didn't live in a castle with soldiers watching the walls. We don't know what room is she in. We don't even know how to get in the compound. Even if we got in without being noticed, we'd have to drop several guards with silencers or crossbows or longbows, which we don't have. Then we'd need night vision goggles, which we don't have. And if we pulled all this off, we'd have to travel at night in Nuevo. Then you have the lake problem; the boat guy has to maneuver at night, and good luck with that. It has to be during the day and quiet."

"Shit, Toño, why don't we just knock on the door and ask for sugar pants?"

"Now that would work, Paco—just go up and ask for 'la mas puta,' and they'll just hand her over with a big grin to pass the day? Listen, guys, this is really serious shit. We don't get this ruka out of Nuevo Laredo, we are done, finito, toast. Comprenden?"

Jay stands up, and as serious as his movie likeness, he says, "Let's get a double for her and pass her off as the real one. I know guys at the Dallas Cowboys that can dress up and look like any chick, honest."

Rigo leans back and starts in, "Dude you go to the fags' whorehouse?"

We all start laughing, except for Jay.

54

Jay yells, "Not that way, putos."

"Worry about the bridge first, then we will worry about a double, Jay."

5

THE BRIDGE

The bridge isn't as busy as it used to be, because of all the killings and kidnappings. The only people that cross now are the truly poor folks who have nothing, the players who have meets with drug runners or hitters looking for workers from the US. We don't fit that profile, but we're crossing with Jay, who is known. That should be enough to get us in without eyebrows raising.

"This guy of yours, Jay—can you trust him?"

"No, but that's all we got."

I hate driving into Nuevo. It's so scary, with everyone turning on their own. You can't trust anybody or anything.

We drive over to the Indio bar in downtown Laredo to pick up the car with the concealed compartments.

Downtown Laredo used to be a thriving area with a colorful busy square. It actually had three movie theaters: the Plaza, the Tivoly, and the Azteca, all blocks from each other. First movie I ever saw was *Jungle Book* at the Plaza. It had green, crushed velvet curtains and deer and rabbits and shit painted on the ceiling. The movie wasn't bad. Now, all the businesses are closed and it's a ghost town.

We get to it—it's backed up to the back end of the building. Rigo and Paco get out and canvas the area to make sure the coast is clear. We check out the car and start loading up all our shit. It's an old classic Chevy Nova with all the cutouts for our gear. The cutouts are made as a second floor in the car. If you look at it from the bottom it looks normal, but a second floor was made to hide all your guns and ammo. Jay pulls the two grenades out of his pants and hangs them over the rearview mirror with a piece of leather. Genius—they look like ornaments. Nobody in their right mind would think they're real.

We pull out and check the blinkers and lights to make sure we don't get pulled over by any cops on the way. You can't leave anything to chance.

Last year, I was running a large bag from Houston to Fort Worth. A buddy of mine was going to meet me downtown by Cantina Laredo for the exchange. I had an old Dodge Cummings diesel truck that made more noise than a busted chainsaw. A Fort Worth cop pulled me over two blocks from the restaurant for a taillight not working—a fucking taillight. One thing I know is if it was in Laredo or neighboring towns, I could have talked my way out of it. But not these big city cops; they are really good. He asks me for my driver's license and insurance, so I give him my license but not my insurance. I do this so if he has a quota or needs to write tickets, he has one for sure and will leave me alone.

Well, he calls for a backup and they ask me to exit my truck. I say, "No." He says, "Why not?" I tell the cop I have a bad left knee and it's hard for me to stand up. He yells with that authoritarian voice, "What you doing in *my town*, boy?" I drop my head and with a meek voice say, "I'm here to fuck your wife. She's the best!" They both take a step back and look at each other, then just start laughing and shoving each other like two kids in a playground. "Boy, I know you're not talking about my wife. She is horrible in bed." We all have a laugh and he lets me off with a warning. Always make sure your car is in tip-top shape.

We start driving up to the old bridge, and I can't help but get that familiar rock in my gut. Shit, this sucks, but let's get ready. If Jay's guy crosses us, we might have to blow past the bridge and hope the Mexican side isn't ready to repel us.

"Jay, which lane is your guy in?"

"I don't know. I can't see him." Jay cranks his neck out the window like he's a goddamn pit bull. "He's in the middle lane. Move over, Toño. Hurry, before they eye us moving around."

"Oh shit, oh shit, I can't get over. Fuck it. I'm stuck."

A cop is waving us up into the left one."

"We are fucked, Toño," Rigo says with a smile, even though he looks worried as piss.

"We need to get in. Jay, do your thing—talk to the cop."

Jay leans over between Toño and the steering wheel. "Hey, compa, we are just going to have a couple of beers at El Papa Gallo. Want to come with us?"

This cop peers in the car and looks at Jay, the famous pachuco, going to Nuevo Laredo to drink tequila and screw women.

"Fuck no I don't want to go with all you guys. Don't forget to wear a rubber, dumbasses."

"Ha!" Jay yells, "Okay, bro, have a nice day, osifer."

"Keep smiling for the cameras, boys, till we get to the middle of the bridge. They have cameras watching us till the Mexican half."

"That was easy, Toño. Don't you think? Wasn't it?"

"Was it, Rigo?" We got lucky, and I will take luck over skill anytime.

"Okay, guys," I whisper, "we still need to get by the Mexicans. I just hope we don't get the red light and get checked.

Jay says, "Dude, if we get red lighted, we will have to blow by and make a run for it…. Move to the last lane—I know that guy. Just do it."

"Okay, Jay, I'll pull up to the short Mexican cop. The guy looks like he's slept in his uniform for the last month."

I hate to stereotype, but this guy is as true as they come. Picture a five-foot-nothing, roly-poly, round-face Tijuana cop in a dirty brown uniform with his waist about two feet from the ground and a rusted-out revolver with pearl grips. I mean, he is straight out of a Cantinflas movie.

"Jay, I hope he's a compa and won't fuck us," I add.

"Nombre, it's cool bro. Just pull up."

The cop waddles up on my side and asks in Spanish what we're doing coming into his town. I turn and look at Jay.

Jay starts with his vato talk. "Hey, bro, it's me, Jay. You remember me? We are just going to El Gallo for some fun, so let us through."

"Pinche Jay, you owe me money from the last time I let you cross."

"I'll pay you later."

"I'll pay you later, my ass," the cops yells.

"Oye, who you think you're talking to?"

Jay, dude, take it easy. "Official, what does Jay owe you?"

"It was fifty, but because he hasn't paid me, it's a hundred."

60

"A hundred?" Jay says with a grunt. "Are you kidding me, a hundred?"

"Jay, I got this, bro."

"Look, let's make it sixty for the bother," Jay continues. "If we pay any more, we won't have enough for the whores and tequila. Tu entiendes como es la cosa."

"Bueno. Ochenta y ya."

"Okay, official, eighty. But you're cutting into our fun."

"Get the fuck out of here, putos," the cop says, counting his money.

I do as the cop says and get the fuck outta there.

"Toño, why did you bargain with that jura?" Paco asks.

"If I would have just pulled a cino out, he would have 1) known we had money and shaken us down hard, or 2) hauled us in and had his buddies squeeze us to find out what we are up to. No, we had to play the part of a few bros going to the whorehouse with little money to party."

Jay is pissed. He doesn't like my reasoning. I can see the steam coming out his ears.

"But why the fuck you pay him $80 for? Eighty? He ripped us off."

"Jay, I understand the principle, but we are loaded down with guns and ammo, and two grenades hanging from our rearview mirror. So it's okay, calm down."

Seems that excuse is working for him. Jay shuts up for now.

MONTEZUMA

"**P**uta madre, that was way too close. I think I shit myself," Rigo says.

"You and Paco get together on how the hell we get out alive from the Montezuma Bar. They're going to pat us down real good. The only one known in the bar is Jay, and if they take his gun, we are fucked."

"Toño, why the hell they pat anybody down? Everyone inside are badass killers and crooks."

"Shit, Rigo. Tell him, Jay."

"Because they want to make sure if anything is going to happen, it's them doing the killing."

"What does our guy with the skinny on the girl look like?" I ask Jay.

"Yeah, he has a big head, like really big. Dude, they cut his hair by the acre. The guy sleeps sitting up. If not, his water head will leak and drown his ass."

"Shit, Jay, you should have stopped before that one," Rigo says.

"Fuck you, Rigo. Pinche puto jerkoff."

"Now that's funny, Jay."

It's my turn to set the plan. "Jay, here is the skinny. You go in and do your thing, and we will follow thirty minutes later. That big head dude better be in the bar when we go in. If they find your pistol, we'll be floating in the wind. And Jay, do your vato pachuco thing and get in with the quete."

Jay nods and steps out and walks to the bar with his pachuco walk.

"Thirty minutes before we go in after Jay?" Rigo asks.

"Yeah. What's the problem?"

"That puto will be all fucked up by the time we get in. I've seen Jay down a whole bottle of mescal plus a six-pack in that time."

"Rigo, he will keep it together. Remember, he owes me."

"Why didn't you remind him before he left?"

"It's his responsibility now to remember, not mine. He's old school and a pachuco to the bone. Now, you two get your mind right before we go into that shithole they call a bar."

The Montezuma is a killer's paradise that's been in the Bass family for fifty years. The Basses are from Mexico— they're not gringos, as most people think, and I would not bring it up even as a joke. They have no sense of humor when it comes to family. It's said old man Bass was on the run from the Mob in Chicago back in the sixties for a hit he made on a rival boss. Old man Bass ended up in Monterrey, Mexico. He married a whore from El Pullman whorehouse at La Zona in Nuevo Laredo. La Zona is a compound on the outskirts with a bunch of whorehouses. The place has a white wall surrounding it, and one way in or out. You fuck up there, you don't leave but tits up.

Anyway, old man Bass started working for the drug runners. They weren't even cartels yet, just small-time marijuana runners. He cut a lot of competition out for his crew; they say the bodies he buried during those days are the foundation the cartels stand on today. The old man had two sons. Being brought up by a killer and a whore will make you a success in the drug cartel society, and they grew up to be even worse than the old man. The brothers took over the Montezuma when he died. Everyone knows if you get out of line, you end up in one of the 55-gallon drums they have in the basement of the bar. These drums are half-full of acid, and a welder sits next to them waiting to seal in whoever the brothers see fit to stuff inside—and those people are not always dead. They usually have around six barrels on Thursday, but if you go by Monday, you might find three or four left. I don't even want to think about that shit with the pull we have to do.

Thirty minutes go by slow when you're waiting in an alley outside the Montezuma. Nuevo has a smell like no other place in the world. It's a wet, ominous feeling like you get in a cellar or dungeon. It's hard to wash off Nuevo Laredo. So we sit and keep an open eye for any wannabe carjackers with no idea who we are or how we're armed. Can you imagine a guy with a revolver trying to hold us up, and all three of us pull out our hardware? It would be worth it just to see his face—or around here, her face.

Time's up, and we hide our pistols and shotguns back in the cutout compartments. We walk up to the monster door of the bar. There's no name on the place, just an old, heavy, weathered, wooden door. Minus the flashy green paint, it looks all medieval and shit. You can sense the pain on the other side. We knock and hear five locks release—two turn like usual, one is really a latch, and two are deadbolts. I got an ear for locks.

The door opens and a couple bouncers look us over. They let us into a small landing area and pat us down. I'm not feeling too good about this, but we're holding our own. They point at a narrow hallway that leads to dark, steep stairs. It feels like the entrance to hell—just a guess. I hear the bouncers securing the five locks above us—well, the four locks and one latch. A cold chill runs down my back. You see, the locks aren't to keep people out, but to keep them in.

We make the bottom of the stairs and knock on the second door. A piece of wood slides open at eye level. This is where you state your name and business. I tell the guy— who's just a pair of beady little eyes looking at me at this point—"I'm here to see Jay. My name is Toño, and this is my crew." The doorman looks over his shoulder at one of the Bass brothers. We're trapped here; if we don't get the nod, we could be done and gone. The brother walks over to the hole in the door. Well, we aren't getting a nod from the brother, and the doorman is getting nervous. This one is the younger and meaner of the brothers. He looks at me like a tiger looks at a steak. I hope he doesn't recognize me from the Jay incident years back. I look him dead in his green eyes and say, "Hey, Bass, how you doing?"

Little Bass whispers, "In here, no piece of work or actions. You hear me, Toño? Yeah, I know who you and your uncle are. As long as you don't have El Machete with you, come in."

The door opens and Little Bass continues, "That fucking dude was here a while back and killed a guy with a plate of nachos."

"Nachos? Yeah, I heard about it, Bass."

"No. With a fucking plate of nachos."

66

"I heard he smashed him across his face with the plate like it was a fucking cream pie and broke his fucking neck," Rigo says, even though no one was talking to him.

Little Bass shakes his head. "Cause of him I have to use paper plates. I hate that dude."

"I'll let him know you said that, Bass," I say with a nervous laugh.

"Okay, mind your manners or 55."

"Yeah, I get it. We'll be in and out before you know it."

"Fuck you, Toño. Come on in with your guys."

It's so dark we can barely see the bar. We walk up to the bartender, basically feeling our way, doing a Helen Keller. Up close, I can see the bartender is an old river rat with scared eyes. In here, you can't blame him. I shit you not, this is the most dangerous bar—most dangerous place—in Mexico. And you can feel it.

The old geezer nods and even smiles, which is odd—a smile. He's toothless. That makes more sense, for some damn reason.

Rigo asks for a Heiny—a fucking Heineken in the Montezuma. I jump in, laugh, and order three Carta Blancas and three tiros de tequila.

"Rigo, Heiny? Here? What the fuck? You and Paco go find Jay and the big head."

The bartender places the drinks on the bar and says, "Sixty."

I turn and look at him like he's fucking crazy.

He says, "Pesos, pendejo."

I crack a smile and throw him 100 pesos. I let him keep the change—just because we are from Zapata doesn't mean you can't tip big (even though we're not known as good tippers). If you're in this bar, you're a noise somewhere, and therefore have money.

Just as I was about to shove my Bed Stu boot up Rigo's ass for not following orders, I hear a voice yell "Jotos!" All I see is Jay stumbling toward us with a bottle of mescal in his hand.

Rigo whispers, "Thirty minutes, dude, thirty minutes. I told you."

Jay walks right up to the bar and drinks all three of our tequila shots. He's laughing and hugging us like a drunk in a whorehouse.

"Come to the table, pendejos." Jay stumbles off into the dark side of the room.

As we head to the table, we can catch a look of the clientele. I swear it looks like the *Star Wars* cantina scene. True Mexican types with looks of grit and hate. Some look so crazy fronting and maxing their toughness, they look like aliens from planet I Don't Give a Shit. These guys are not to be trifled with, by any means. In the corner of the bar, we see this guy with the biggest head ever to sit on top a Mexican's shoulders. I have never seen anything like it outside of a circus. His eyes are wide open, as if to say, "Please help me."

I sit next to Jay, lean close, and whisper, "You better be acting drunk."

Jay sits back and gives me a wink.

I start in with Big Head. "You have the information we need on this chick?"

B.H., with his scared, wide-eyed look, replies, "I don't have shit to say until money hits my hand, putos."

I have to explain to him how this works. He tells us what we need to know first. Then, and only then, will we hit him with the money. That's how it works. B.H. finds some guts somewhere—maybe he's got an extra fifty feet or so jammed between his ears. God knows there's room.

"I don't care what you guys say. I want my money up front. What you guys are trying to do will not only get you killed, but worse than that, will get my ass dropped."

"Do you or don't you know what we need to know? I'm not going to ask you twice, entiendes."

"Yes, I know all about that ruka. I used to help El Commandante by doing all the yard work. I used to peek into her bedroom when I was weed whacking, and I know everything she does. A lotta weeds growing up by her window. That shit took hours to whack off, if you know what I mean. I know things."

Pinche pervert piece of shit. "I need to know what you know."

"I had a hand to play on this squirt to get him to give up the information."

"Big Head, this is not the place to do business. If the Bass brothers catch a whiff of what we're doing here, we will be leaving in a 55-gallon tank, and you know it. And you'll be leaving in two, sliced in half at the neck. So get your mind right. You think we don't take prisoners? Get up if you can with that head of yours. Let's step outside."

"No fucking way, putos, I'm staying here. Jay says you need this intel about her and Commandante, so fuck you, and you, and 'specially you, Jay."

The quiver in Big Head's voice is clear like a glass of stale beer that's been baking in the sun. Still, shit for brains thinks he has a good hand in the game.

"Look, B.H.," I clamor in.

"Toño, who's B.H?"

"This fucker here. Big Head, stupid. Stay up on the conversation, Rigo. Look—you have two choices, B.H. Die here, or walk outside with us."

"Fuck you, whoever you are. I know you can't have a quete in this place."

"My name is Toño. And really? Then what's this Glock sticking you in your balls?"

I wasn't just whispering to Jay earlier, but getting the pistol handed to me.

"A la verga, you motherfucker," B.H. says.

I had to set him straight. "Motherfucker, say one more thing about my mother. I dare you, I double-dare you, ese."

"Sorry, sorry. It just slipped. I know no mother shit."

70

"Okay, B.H. You want to die for information or get paid for it, stupid?"

"Okay. Pay me first, Toño, or I won't go."

"Get the fuck up, you fucking water head. Andale."

B.H. gets up with my Glock in his ribs. The crew follows. Those twenty yards to the door by the stairs are the hardest. We start on the stroll, and every one of the fifteen guys in the bar is watching the walk with curiosity. They know a play is on, but aren't sure if it's sanctioned by the brothers, so they stay out of it. Interfering with the Bass brothers' business for any reason will get you dropped, and these regulars know when to stay and when to play. Now I know what the dead men walking in Huntsville Prison feel like.

B.H. begins to look frantically for either of the Bass brothers as we get to the door. I move to the side and block his view to salvation. I remind him that the Bass brothers will kill him and us—him for snitching and us for working a snatch on their turf.

"I haven't snitched and you know it, Toño."

"Try telling them that, B.H. If they don't understand it, they kill it. It's their code."

As the front door opens and sunlight shines on us, it feels like the parting of the Red Sea. Once outside, Jay bitchslaps B.H. a little for the fuck of it and stuffs him in the car.

"Jay, drive us to the south toward Monterrey and cut off to the left as soon as you get outside of town. There's a shed we've used before. We need some quiet time with B.H."

About two miles outside Nuevo Laredo, we pull into the shed. It's a wreck—rotting wood, dirt floor, at least a hundred years old.

As soon as we get B.H. out of the car, he starts blabbing about the girl's movements, her habits, the cars she's been driving. He tells us she goes to the coffee shop across the street every day to get sweetbread around three in the afternoon. We get what we need before we even sit his wide ass and big head down, but this dude will not shut the fuck up. I mean, the color of her dresses, the shoes she wears. How she pulls her hair to the side. It got so bad, I thought Jay was going to strangle him with his bare hands.

When B.H. finally takes a break to breathe, I say, "You guys stick this blabbermouth in the trunk. Jay, drive this fuck to El Malibu whorehouse and have Lola keep him on ice until we're done with our thing. Give her these 500 clams to give him a good time—but tell her not to untie him, cause he will sell us out."

"500?" Jay balks.

"Shit, Toño, that's a pretty good time," Rigo adds.

7

UNSUSPECTED AND UNDETECTED

Well, we have a window of opportunity for the snatch with the information B.H. gave us. Every day she goes for coffee and sweetbread across the street from El Commandante's compound.

"Toño, how you see this working out, homes? They have twenty vatos with quernos." Collapsible-stock AK-47s.

I yell out, "Swing arm!"

"What?" Jay asks.

"Swing arm, Jay."

"Okay, Toño, I know the only school I went to was gladiator school in Huntsville, but I don't get it."

"We did one of these in Freer, Texas a while back, when we snatched El Popo. I'll explain later. Jay, we need that river rat on the river pointing east and ready to go all the way to San Ygnacio."

"Okay. I'll double check on it and make him know what's what if he doesn't show. I'll press him. I know where his jefita and kids live on the US side."

"Rigo and Paco, go find us a working van with a sliding door, a can of grease or a grease gun, twenty-five feet of thick rope that can handle 500 pounds. Also, get some bandanas for you guys. I have my own."

Paco shakes his head. "Toño, dude, everybody knows you carry your lucky red Lone Star bandana. I'll get you a different bandana, bro."

"Didn't think about that. Don't need to slip now on a stupid oversight."

I have used my red Lone Star Beer bandanas ever since I was in Bandera, Texas during the Whataburger race-horse finals. My tio had a horse in the eighth race. I was the guy that would stand in front of the stall to cover my tio's trainer while he shot up the horse with a syringe in the neck. Don't judge me—it's what you did in these dirt tracks just to compete.

The guy running the book was behind the stands, next to the concessions. Well, I made my bet after the horse cocktail, and turned around to buy a Lone Star beer. This good-looking gal asked me if I had a horse in the running.

I said of course. She said if my horse won, she would give me her favorite red Lone Star bandana—the one around her neck. The horse won by a nose, and wasn't disqualified for the doping due to the flush injection given to him in the winner's circle. Well, I went to get my prize. Two months later, I brought her back to Bandera. And what a two months it was. Every time I touch that bandana, I think of sweet Lolita.

"Rigo, whacha oversight! Todo, mammon!"

Jay is suddenly full of wise cracks. At least we're not all nerves. We have to get this done or everything else doesn't matter. As Jay takes off with B.H., Rigo and Paco go get the van and all the stuff. I start getting that bad feeling again. I just can't figure out a way not to get dead on delivering this chick. What the fuck is the out? There's always an out...just have to find it.

My phone vibrates, and it's my valley boys with info that might save or bury us. What they start laying on me feels like a slow, hard kick to the balls. I need to have them say it three times and I still can't believe it. Now with this information, I might figure out how to flip this to our advantage—like El Machete did with the nacho plate. But I don't want to get ahead of myself. There are plenty of ways to cut up a whore; I just need to find the one.

I make my phone calls and say my prayers in record time, maybe just too short to work out a lifeline. Fuck 'em. That Tio thinks he's untouchable because of his contracts with the big boys in Mexico. Well, let's see how loyal they really are. Nut cutting time, and I will be holding the knife. I just hope I don't cut my own nuts off.

8

THE SWING ARM

We have three hours before she makes her walk to the coffee shop. We have to be set up and ready.

"Toño, what is all this shit you had us get?" Paco asks.

"Hold on. Jay, how did it go with B.H.?"

"That puto is going to have a lot more fun than we are. That chick is going to rocket twist him until he goes blind."

"Nombre, you tell her anything?"

"No way, just her job."

"Okay, I know what to expect from her."

"What does that mean?"

"Nothing, Jay. You did good, thanks."

"Rigo, Paco—take everything out of the van, it smells like an outhouse. Does this piece of shit run?"

"Oh yeah, it runs good. Topped it off with petrol. The tires are okay, and the brakes kind of work, but it's the best we could find."

"Okay, Toño, what the hell is the grease and heavy rope for?" Rigo asks. "You can't tie up a girl with the thick rope like that."

"The grease is for the sliding door. It can't make a sound. The rope will be tied to the van with just enough slack to let me dangle just outside the door. When she crosses the street, Jay will drive close to her on the right side. The door opens, I lean out to grab her on the move, pull her in in quietly, close the door, and we bail. All in all, three seconds from start to finish. By the time anybody says anything, we'll be halfway to the boat."

"Shit, Toño! That's simple, smooth, and the van blocks the guards' view. She's there one second and gone the next. Wow, I have to give it to you, dude, that's brilliant."

"Thanks, Jay, but let's not start jerking each other off just yet. We have two hours. Let's get everything ready and set up, dale shine."

I didn't want to say anything about what the Valley boys found out, or what could happen to the guys if we don't pull this off. I need them frosty and on point. This swing arm has to get done or we are fucked. I got the phone calls made while they worked on the van.

This slice of work I'm laying down has to be cut with a sharp knife, thin, fast, and perfect. No room for mistakes. If these guys think I'm playing them, it won't work. I have to have the girl to make the play for all of us to survive, including Jay. He might think he isn't in the big mix, and I hate to slide him in the picture. I needed him to get the job done. Sorry, bro, but it had to be done. The good thing is, he knows the game. Hell, he was in the game at age nine. The play has to stay with me or it won't work. I know my guys; they will pick it apart and make a play for my tio.

They don't know him like I do. He has all the angles worked out. He probably has eyes on us now. Shit, he might take us right after we snatch the girl and leave us floating on the Rio Grande as fish bait. That dude thinks five steps ahead and when he comes, it's quick and ruthless. I'm going to play a hand I hope he hasn't seen or expects. Life on the border is unlike anyplace else in the world. Nobody breaks the boss's rules, because if you do, you pay the price. I'm going against everything I was taught my whole life, but I have an edge in this game. I know my tio has to kill us to save his own ass. Knowing this one thing changes the game. *He* broke the rule first— the cardinal rule.

There is nothing like having your own blood dust your ass, and for what? Money and power. Fuck that dude. His time is up for the action he's trying to pull. There is an old saying in Mexico: *"El diablo save mas por viejo que por diablo."* The devil knows more because he is old, than because he is the devil. Today, Tio is just getting old, with no devil left in him.

Time to change the direction of the tide. Time to stack the chips high on our side.

9

THE DRAG

"Okay, we have the van ready, Rigo?"

"Yeah, the door is slicker than a frog's hair. All you have to do is check the length of the rope for your lean."

As I tie the rope around my waist, I'm hoping it's not going to be around my neck later. "Perfect, Rigo. Tie it down and make sure it doesn't slip."

We load up. I really want to spill the entire plan to the guys, but I can't. I have to play it out as is. I really love these guys. Jay, just like in a big brother way, but they're a true crew. Honor, loyalty—this you just can't find much of on the border. It's like looking for a Mexican on a ski slope.

Setting up without being noticed by El Commandante's crew won't be easy, but it's 2:00 p.m. in the middle of Nuevo Laredo. The streets will be busy, which will give us the edge we need to go undetected. I hope. We start loading up in the van. We all look at each other with slight nods of confidence.

We drive to the location of the snatch. The streets are hot. You can smell the desperation in the air from the majority of Mexican citizens begging for a break in life. Shit, man. A few more miles south, and I could have been born in Mexico, stuck here in the mix. I thank God from time to time for letting me be born a Tex-Mex and not a Mex-Mex.

I tell Jay to pull into that parking spot by a truck.

"Why the truck, Toño? I can't see."

"It will give us cover until the pull."

The guys are nervous and tense and frosty—like they should be.

"Jay, can you turn the radio on?"

"What? People will notice us with the music playing."

"I know, that's what we want. Not four guys in a van looking nervous. Turn it on."

The radio cracks on, and the one and only Augustin Lara is singing on the Mexican station.

"This guy was the coolest cat back in the day," Jay announces. "I think he killed himself with heroin, but his music is badass."

"Toño, this better work or a la verga—we are fucked," Rigo whispers.

"It will, just handle the door. And Rigo—when I pull her in, you make sure she doesn't make a sound."

"How the hell am I supposed to do that? I have never hit a girl, and I'm not starting now."

"Rigo, just wrap your legs around her from behind and use both hands to cover her mouth. Be gentle-like and whisper in her ear, 'We are not going to hurt you.' And tell her she is going to be okay, over and over."

"Okay, but I don't want to hurt a girl."

"That's why you are handling the chick, Rigo. If she's hurt in any way, we could be dropped in a deep hole."

Waiting for the front doors of the hacienda to open is the hardest part so far. Shit, here she comes. "She's not alone, guys."

"We are fucked, Toño. What the fuck are we going to do now?" Rigo asks. "Wait. Look, the maid is going the other way from the coffee shop."

"See, I told you guys it would be okay." I smile and shake off the stress that just came out of my body like beer in a sauna.

"Damn, she is good-looking, homes," Paco says.

"You think they would want an ugly girl, pendejo? Jay—pull out slowly, and when she's in the middle of the street, let her walk by with a wave and a big smile."

Wow, this chick is perfect—long black hair and a body to die for. Her eyes are green like the color of money. Green eyes are rare on the border—not like the interior of Mexico, but that's another story. I can't imagine what they look like up close. Probably glow in the fucking dark. We are about to find out.

I had a girl like her as a girlfriend once. She was from Rio Grande City, Texas. A meaner girl you could not find, but a looker. Her dad was the sheriff, which meant he was a bigger crook than we are. I really loved that chick, but like I said, she was crazy. Her dad got arrested for using his prisoners to move coke from Mexico to Houston. Her family had a ton of drug money saved up, so they move to Oklahoma. She asked me to follow her and leave this life behind. I couldn't leave my jefita, and what would my tio do? That's what I told her. Truth is, I'm not into mean, complicated women with killer left hooks. And who wants to live in Oklahoma? It makes South Texas look like Miami. She left and last I heard, she married a pig farmer in Tulsa. I hope that pork-chop-eating bastard makes her crazy ass happy.

As soon as she crosses the van, we pull forward. Paco opens the door nice and quiet as Jay inches the van ahead and veers right. I lean out of the side and grab her by the

84

waist. As I start pulling her in, I squeeze her stomach as to exhale her breath so she can't scream. Well, as you can imagine, something goes wrong—she collapses like dead weight, and dead weight is heavier and harder to hold onto. We start to drive off, dragging her down the street, but just like a hawk dives in to catch a fish, Paco grabs the girl from in front of me—around the left side—and pulls her in the van. The door slams shut, and off we go. We look back. El Commandante's boys are nowhere to be found. They saw nothing. Somebody is going to get killed from that crew.

"Take it easy, Jay," I say.

Like a Sunday driver, he putts down the shitty streets of Nuevo Laredo in a van with a hostage.

"Cover her up and tape her mouth and hands, Rigo. And let's get the fuck out of town."

I notice this chick is staring into my eyes with a look of desperation—sort of what you would see in a snitch's eyes when he's tied to a chair with El Machete standing over him, but you've heard that story.

I dive toward her, face to face, and whisper, "You're okay. We aren't going to hurt you if you just shut up and do as you're told. Comprendes? Blink if you understand, penda."

She blinks. I see that fear in her eyes turn into fucking hate. "Rigo, ease up a bit on the grip. She's starting to look pissed. We don't know you and don't want to know you.

So button up and be cool, and you will be okay. I promise. We won't touch you, you know, like that. But if you try to run or give us away, I'll hit you so hard you will shit your pants."

Rigo starts to loosen up the grip on this fine chick and the fight is on. Rigo grabs her around the mouth again and Paco pulls the duct tape—round and round it goes, hands, feet, and a piece across her mouth.

Something's not right. She's wearing Versace jeans, a Vera Wang top, and a badass A. Lange & Sohne 18-karat red gold watch. Now, I have only seen these bad boys on movie stars and big noises. It's a status thing in the drug world. Hell, I hide my Submariner around those guys due to embarrassment. I want to ask her some questions, but we need to get the hell out of the piranha pit first.

10

THE TURN

"Jay, I have a twist. Turn right toward Monterrey."

"What! Dude, I have the guy waiting in the boat by the river to get us the fuck out of here."

"I have something working. Think about it—our exit has always been fucked."

"What do you mean, Toño? It's all set up," Rigo says.

"That's right. It's set up for an ambush. Do you really think my tio hasn't been ready for anything we got planned? You think he hasn't had his boys watching us? We go to the boat, we're done right there."

"How do you know that?"

"Because, Rigo, that's what I would do. And just in case, I had Big Head let go before we made the pull. By now, everybody knows we have the girl. The boat waiting for us also has Tio or El Commandante's boys waiting for us."

"Toño, we are dead and you killed us, you mother-fucker!" Jay yells.

"I have planned this, and we have an out. We were going to be floaters anyway we turned."

"You lied to us, after all this bullshit. You fucked us."

"Jay, just drive to Monterrey. They will never think of that. We buy some time to work a deal out that doesn't end with us getting dead."

Jay slams on the breaks. We're two miles out of Nuevo Laredo. He jumps out of the van. I know what's next—he's going to kill me right here.

"Rigo, Paco, cover me from Jay and I promise I'll get us out of this."

Rigo and Paco get their guns up and cocked before I finish my sentence.

Jay walks around the van. He's going for the sliding door. He's got his hand on the latch. I'm staring at Rigo and Paco with a smile. Goddamn, I love my boys. The door flies open. Jay has his pistol in his hand with this blank look on his face. Well, it's not so much blank as the kind of look you'd see in a person who has no soul. This is the point where I have nothing left but to do but trust in my guys. Just like clockwork, Rigo and Paco draw a bead with their pistols and cover Jay.

Jay starts yelling, "I'm gonna kill you, puto. You killed me. You fucking killed me."

Rigo explains, "Jay, drop the gun, or I will make a canoe out of your head."

Paco just quietly holds his revolver, cocked and ready, and looks at Jay with those happy fucking eyes.

Me, I'm looking at the girl with my finger on my lips so she stays quiet and still, so as not to cause a bloodbath. Tense is the moment. Death might be coming for a visit, and all it needs is a whisper. Jay is a true killer, not like us. We do what we have to. Jay enjoys it. Time freezes and everything else slows down to a crawl.

The only thing I can do now is sweat out a low-pitch statement. "I have a plan. Now, we can start the killing, but who wants to die in Nuevo Laredo?"

Jay stares me down like a statue.

This can go either way right now, and so be it. My problem has just become threefold. There's the main issue: my tio. Jay's considering dropping me dead. And I can't stop staring at the groovy watch that chick is wearing. I'm going to have to get me one of those, if this all plays out and we stay alive.

Jay slowly lowers his pistol down to his thigh.

Here is where Rigo and Paco earn their reputation of being savvy to the underworld. They don't move their sights off Jay. You give a guy like Jay an inch, he will raise his gun and kill us all, including the girl.

"Orale, Jay. Let the gun slide to the ground, and I promise if you don't like the deal I'm going to lay out, I'll take the girl on my own. You know me—I've done most of the planning for my tio the last four years. He has us dead and you know that, homes, you've been around. Let it slide, Jay. Just do it."

As I see the gun hit the ground, I'm still worried. Jay is quick. He could pull another pistol.

Rigo and Paco don't move. They still have a bead on Jay, like good seasoned soldiers.

"Time to come clean. Times have changed for guys like us. We serve. We die or end up in jail. Jay, you know this better than most. You have pulled a lot of time for these putos and you kept your mouth shut. For what? These guys don't give a shit about you and they're ready to drop us in a hole. For what? Pinche money."

"Don't you think I know what I am and who I'm working for? You think your telling me something new? I signed up for this as a kid because I was living in the streets, stealing food for me and my sister. Why do you care about me? Don't do that for me. It's just too late. We finish this job and we're square. But if you lie to me again, I will finish it without you."

"Jay, I care about all of us because we will be you in ten years, God willing. And nothing personal, but I plan to change the game and save our own souls. You know, if we don't, who will?"

For the first time, there is understanding on Jay's face and a calm I have never seen.

Rigo asks Jay to raise his shirt, just in case he has a hideout. Jay looks at Rigo with a *fuck you, I'm a pachuco* attitude.

I sit up from the van between Rigo and Paco. "Jay, follow the command, or it ends here on this dirt road in fucking Mexico."

Jay nods and raises his shirt; we all see he has a .38 in his waist. He smiles and gives us all props for a job well done.

Paco takes the tape off the princess's mouth to let her breath a bit. She is smart enough to see she's in the middle of rattlers that want to swallow each other whole, so she quietly sits back and takes in the show.

Me, I'm fucking sweating it up waiting for the next act. I have to run down the plan to these guys, and I really have to sell it, or I might end up in a hole right here in Old Mexico.

11

THE STORY

"You guys remember the guy we floated in South Padre island?"

"Yeah, that's why we are here sweating bullets."

"Well, my tio said that puto was the son of his connection in Mexico, who wanted us dead. He also said he worked out this snatch to get us right and save us from Mexico killing us. I reached out to some guys that owe me from that thing in Brownsville several years back. They called me while you guys were getting the stuff for the van. They said that kid I floated wasn't the son of his Mexico connection, but a mule for the cartel bringing 100 kilos of coke. He stored the coke in my tio's stash house in Harlingen the night before he had to deliver it. They say my tio stole the 100 kilos of coke, and when the mule was blaming my tio about the missing coke, Tio gave me up as the thief—even told him I was his kin as to make it more believable to the Mexican Cartel. He also said where I was going to be that night, knowing they would kill me."

"Toño, why would your tio do that? He made you his number one guy. He trusts you will his money and family."

"Paco, the last two years, I've been manning the drug running for him—the whole enchilada. He's been drinking way too much and talking a lot more. So much, everybody knows his business, and I think it got back to Mexico's ears. I don't want his damn job and I've told him that, but he's gotten really paranoid. He thinks they need to replace him with a newer, bigger model—me."

"Shit, Toño, I remember your tio stood with your mom at your high school graduation," Rigo adds.

"My tio groomed me just like a coach conditions an athlete. He saw the talent I had—loyalty, brains, and muscle. He needed me as an asset for his business, someone he could trust and bring up to run and gun for him. The funny thing about this whole bullshit is I just wanted him to be proud of me by doing a good job. Now I see what I am to him—just another ant in the farm, and one that he has to step on.

"You see, I couldn't figure out why that cat came after me for no reason in South Padre. That had been bothering me like a burr under the saddle. If he had killed me, Tio gets away with 100 kilos and you guys get tortured and killed."

"Why would they fuck with us?"

"Well, you're my crew. If you wanted to find the coke, who would you ask? You see, Rigo, that fuck Tio set us up from the beginning. He wants me gone because I know all his business transactions and connections. With me gone, Mexico won't replace him. At least, not in the near future. He also thinks I'd retire him with a bullet in the head. Kill the king's successor and the king rules forever, or something like that. You guys know that's all in his head."

I wait for some kind of acknowledgement from the guys. It seems like they're following.

"And more important, Tio is a greedy bastard and wants that coke money to feed his gambling losses in the Louisiana casinos. Shit, he plays three-card poker and Caribbean poker—worst odds on the planet. He also upped his drinking habit. You know that 'Who Hit John' and gambling don't mix. You guys didn't know that about him, but he is a terrible gambler.

"Mexico is pissed and wants the coke or the money, so they squeezed Tio. Said he's responsible for the stolen dope. Tio worked out this snatch from El Commandante to hold over his head. Tio then tells the story to El Commandante that *we* are the thieves that stole the coke and body-snatched the girl. Well, we did that second thing with the girl. My tio is trying to make it look like we're the ones wanting to have the Mexican Cartel boys waxed because *we're* holding El Commandante's daughter hostage. Tio becomes the middleman between El Commandante and us. Tio saves his girl, but only after Mexico has been massacred. Tio then, as a peace offering, kills us and returns the girl."

The guys are just staring at me like I'm speaking freaking French.

Jay finally speaks up. "It's a smart play for Tio all around. Not only does he take over the Mexican pipeline, he makes nice with El Commandante and keeps the coke."

"Why didn't you tell us sooner?" Rigo asks.

"This pull had to be done. If not, we had no chip to play with. If I had told you guys, it would have fucked up our plan, and I know Jay would fly. Jay, I'm sorry I dragged you into this, but I will make it right and put some serious coin in our pocket. Plus, we will be legends when we pull this shit off."

"Toño, I dropped my pistols because I wanted to, and you fuckers know that. It's easy to die for cats like me. The hardest thing to do is live like we do. I done my time and did some things in the crossbar hotel I'm not proud of, but this shit is over my head. I gotta say, I'm not the smartest soldier, but I know what horse to back on a gamble. Toño, I'm with you—not because of the money or because you saved my ass back in the day, but because you always respected me when others thought I was a simple-minded thug. And for that I owe. I'm in all the way, homes. La Pura Vida."

"Jay, you're an honorable man. A crook and a killer, but your word is good. Better than most."

Rigo and Paco are standing there with what looks like tears in their eyes.

Then Rigo starts in. "Jay, you want a hug?"

For the next two minutes, Jay chases Rigo around the van motherfucking him, calling him everything but a white man.

12

THE PLAN

Sitting in the dirt outside of Nuevo Laredo in the heat, next to a van with a kidnapped chick, is not a fun place to be. But what the hell else we going to do? We have to hash out the plan the best we can, and our thinking caps are on tight as we tailgate.

The guys from the Valley said the Mexico boys are none too happy with my tio. He's a bit scared—scared enough to kill us all.

A quick note about the Valley boys making the call. These guys are the underbelly of the smugglers' world. They are the troopers that get cars ready with trapdoors to transport the drugs, and they use sophisticated communication techniques to keep the cops confused, like using different Mexican dialects. They get the drugs from Mexico to Anyplace, USA. No Johnny Law working interdiction on the roads can understand a word they're saying or pinpoint their location. Did you know there are fifty-two dialects in Mexico? These guys have access to all of them. I would love to see the DEA and all the task force dudes listening to Aztec or Nahuatl on a CB radio.

"I'll tell you one thing—I'm not going to end up in the shed with El Machete. We are going to railroad those fucks, with a lot of luck and help from our Valley friends. First, we have to deliver the girl to El Commandante and Mexico, so I called them about this shit I uncovered."

"What did they say, Toño?" Rigo asks.

"They said enough. They listened, and before they hung up, I told them what Tio did and what we have to trade. Big Head has already informed El Commandante about the snatch and who we are, but this had to be done. That's why I told the whore to let him go—right before the snatch. He did just as I imagined. Predictability is a damn beautiful thing."

"I don't see how El Commandante finding out about the snatch helps."

"The sooner El Commandante finds out about the snatch, the faster we can get a meet with Mexico. And now we have their attention as real players in the game. See, if

Mexico doesn't think El Commandante is in play to kill their asses, we are dead, comprendes? A dead girl means shit to the Mexican Cartel, unless they know El Commandante cares enough about her to do the action. And the truth is, El Commandante has taken out competition many times, and much bigger players than the Mexican Cartel. Remember El Tony from Reynosa? He was twice as big as these chumps! He took that beast out in an afternoon.

"I'm going to broker a deal between Tio's bosses, the Mexican Cartel, and El Commandante. My tio ripped off Mexico for 100 keys of coke—worth $800,000—and then he gives us a story so we can snatch the girl from El Commandante. Tio kills us, hides the girl in a safe house.

"Once my tio has the girl, he's going to use her as collateral to make El Commandante use his soldiers—that are three times bigger than the Mexican Cartel—to kill them. That way, my tio doesn't have to return the coke or worry about Mexico killing his crooked ass. Then, he returns the girl to El Commandante as a peace offering and kills us to show his commitment. And Tio keeps the 100 kilos. You caught that part, right?

"It's only smart to put my tio in a corner between these two hitters. Mexico lost face when my tio broke the rules by stealing from them and wanting to have them whacked."

"Your tio has fucking balls to try a play like this."

"That's your problem, Rigo—you underestimate my tio. I know what he's capable of. Another card I have to play is the coke. I know where it is. He sent Pepe to Houston after the Padre Island hit didn't go well for him. He underestimated my knife skills."

"So, it's in a place in Houston?" Jay asks.

"No, he calls Pepe's ranch in Cuero 'Houston' to throw people off."

"Fucking Tio talks too much when he starts drinking beer in the heat. He's getting old and he knows it."

"So what's going to happen when we go meet with him?" Rigo asks.

"Well, you guys will be somewhere far from Monterrey, and I will meet with Mexico's right hand man, the tall German."

"Dude, you're going to meet with the German?"

"Yeah. I'm excited to meet that guy. I heard he calculates everything. He did the twelve killings—those bodies they found in a hole by Reynosa. That German worked in Colombia during the heyday, for Chavez in Venezuela, and in Cuba during his spare time. Some say he was a Hitler youth—which I think is bullshit, but he is a savage motherfucker. The worry I have is that they're sending the German to lower our guard. If we all show up with the girl, they will kill us. Why not? You guys are going to find a quiet place to hole up and I'll see you guys after the meet. I got one hour to meet them and get back to you. If I'm one second late, you drive off to old Zapata, and a boat will find you. That gives you forty-five minutes to get there, or you swim. If they bite but it runs long, I'll catch up. I'll go back to Nuevo Laredo and cross to the US side. I'll get my truck and drive to the meet at El Mesquite. You guys stay on the Texas side of Zapata Viejo—I don't want to know where. Wait until 11:30 the next day. Drive to the entrance of El Mesquite and wait there."

"What if you don't show?" Rigo asks.

"If I'm not there, I'm gone. Mexico and his boys will meet you, and I hope El Commandante will be there, too, to get his property. Hand the girl over to them and make sure she is in tiptop shape. They'll let you leave to make you think you're safe, and probably hit you when you're clear from El Mesquite. Maybe after the big hill that's about five miles out, by where Rigo killed that twelve-point buck."

"Shit, Toño, we still get killed? Fuck me."

"Relax, Danny Trejo. One mile up, the gate to Gata Orcada Ranch will be unlocked. Drive down to the lake—that takes ten minutes—and a boat will be waiting. He'll take you to El Tigere Island and drop you off on the Mexico side. A car will be waiting for you. It's in mint condition and full of gas."

"Where can we go in Mexico that they won't find us?"

"There's directions in the glovebox. It's a safe place. By the way, I taped all my cash to the backseat, inside the

101

liner. You can't see it or feel it in case the drop guy goes through the car, which I know he will. While you guys were getting all the stuff for the drag, I called some friends to have the car delivered, and I had my maid hand my money to the guy picking you up in the boat. He's placing the instructions and money in the drop vehicle. It will be there waiting. You have to trust me. That's all that's left to this plan."

"Who are these guys dropping the car? And the boat guy, Toño?"

"I'd rather not tell you, just in case they send somebody different to do the drop or the boat guy changes drivers. Things change, bros. But really I want it to be a surprise—it's the safest way—and by then, you'll need it to help you keep going."

"I don't like this cloak and dagger shit. It's not right, bro."

"Jay, trust me and we will get this done."

"Toño, I don't like it. I don't want to run. We live here, bro."

"They won't hurt your family. They're not like my tio. They'll kill you easy, but Mexico and El Commandante now know their families are in play by us snatching the girl, and knowing we're still loose in their blind spot will keep 'em tight and straight. For the first time, they will feel vulnerable. They will do my tio and Machete first, and try to kill us as soon as we clear El Mesquite."

"Why won't they just kill us at El Mesquite?"

"Because they don't want to take the chance of Mexico, El Commandante, or his daughter getting in a crossfire with us. They can handle my tio and El Machete. They have them sewed up. They're prepared for them. With us, they're out in the open with four guys that have beat them in Mexico. They aren't sure what we have planned if we have to get down and dirty. They need us away from El Mesquite and away from the principle player. I've seen them work, and they always protect the big noises like Mexico and Commandante.

"Remember, these guys aren't from here. In Texas, they're out in the open. If they don't get us quick, they will haul ass back to Mexico. Picture a rich guy that has to go to the shit part of town with a ton of money to pay a ransom. The rich guy wants to get in and get out and have the dirty work done after he leaves, simple. That's the Mexico way."

"Toño, you have really thought this shit out," Rigo says. "You are a real jefe."

"When you're thrown into this life, you learn or die. This will work, but you guys have to follow the plan no matter what happens. If we play this out, we will be set for some time. Hell, we might be running the show. I know this is a hard thing to do, splitting off like we are, but this has to be done.

"If I don't show in one hour from the meet with the German, Jay, give me your word you'll leave. If they find you, we are all dead. Both the Mexican Cartel and El Commandante's men will be looking for us, along with all the snitches wanting to get paid a finder's fee."

"Toño, I'll leave your ass right now if you want."

I look at Jay, confident he would, in fact, leave my ass. A true player.

"You guys are family. I promised I wouldn't let you down. Take care of that girl—not a scratch, or it could change the deal. I have to meet the German, so I don't want to know where you're going or where you're staying in Zapata Viejo, in case I get asked hard. You guys will be okay. Jay, drop me off at the corner. Don't go by taxi stands or police stations—all eyes are out looking."

"You're an asshole, Toño," Paco says with a smile.

We all laugh, then I hop out.

"I wish he wasn't leaving."

"What did you say, chica? What do you care about Toño?"

"Well, if you must ask, shorty, I was hoping he would be around when you get caught and get your asses beat like redheaded stepchildren."

Paco looks at her. "'Shorty'? And who is redheaded here, pendeja? You're about as dumb as a sack of hammers!"

"Kiss my ass, mini me!"

The van drives away. I walk the streets of Monterrey, Mexico looking for a cab to get me downtown to La Ancira Hotel for the meet. I start to feel the loneliest I have ever felt. I have to pull this trick on my own. No backup; just my wits and balls, which I can feel around my throat right about now.

13

THE MEET

As I jump in a cab, I keep thinking—how long can we hide from these guys? I have to play the hand I laid out. It's the smart play, but thin...very thin. I have five minutes to get to the hotel and meet the German. Driving there, I'm watching all the hardworking Mexicans breaking cement with sledgehammers, carrying fruit, and sweeping the storefronts for pennies a day. I'm lucky to have been born a free Texican, glad to be in my boots. As bad as it is, it could always be worse—broke and living with your head down, staring at the ground you will be buried in. Not me, not today, and certainly not in Monterrey.

I see the hotel. It's a nice place. Again, I feel they will be playing me, so I have to be sharp and act like I know what I'm doing. Before the cab even stops, three guys meet me with big smiles. They're well-dressed in suits and military boots. These guys are in their twenties and in military shape to go with those boots. They don't look like Mexicans look; more like German mercs. They pat me down, still all smiles, and feel me up like they're my close friends—hugs and pats on the back and shit. These guys are good; they found my cold steel knife. The blond one slides it in his front pocket.

"Hey, Guero, I want that knife back, you hear me?"

He smiles with this mischievous look. They take me arm in arm and proceed to walk me into the hotel lobby.

As I'm carried to the elevator, I see this huge Mexican holding the door. This guy is 6'5", 350 lbs., but no belly— a real Tosh hog. They put my back to the elevator wall and stand facing me, chests touching my arms. Any other time, I would make a crack like "Boys, buy me a drink first?" or "You want to dance?" Not these guys; if I flinch, they would pour me into the meeting.

Shit, we're going to the penthouse level—privacy and quiet rooms for whatever they have planned.

As the doors open, another two guys are waiting five feet back. Both are pointing MP5s—submachine guns—at the imaginary bullseye on my forehead. We walk out of the elevator, and one moves toward me, slings his weapon, and begins to pat me down. He's not nice like the other guys; doesn't even say hola. Just like the German to doublecheck everything—these guys are good. Two in front, two in back, they walk me to Suite #8. Finally some luck—eight is my lucky number.

As the door opens, I catch my knees shaking. I clench my hands. Fuck these putos. Let's play.

THE WAIT

Meanwhile back at the van:

"What the fuck, Paco? You ain't the boss."

"I am now, Rigo. I don't want to be, but since Toño is MIA, who else wants to step up?"

"Toño is gone? Paco?"

"He might be taking a dirt nap, ese. Somebody has to steer this fucking trainwreck. You want to drive it, bro, go right ahead."

"Come on, I'm not built for that shit and you know it."

"So why you fucking with me? Step up or get in line, my brother."

"You got anything to add, Jay?"

"Who you think you talking to? I'm Jay, El Pachuco, and I'm here to play. Who the fuck are you—the end of the world?"

"No, just a cat that Toño taught a thing or two to. We gotta get this job done and maybe, just maybe, get out alive with some feria, homes."

"Well, I'm here because of Toño. And he left a trail for us to follow, so I'm in with you. Just don't forget—I'm nobody's 'Hey, boy.'"

"Listen, vatos, I know I usually sit all back of the bus and shit, but I know how Toño thinks, and he left instructions. So we really are still working for him, if that makes you feel better."

These two are tense. Tighter than a bull's ass in fly season. I can sense it. Toño taught me about sensing shit, too.

"Rigo, give the ruka some water."

He looks at me with this smirk of pride—a younger brother watching his own blood do good.

"Bro, just tell the girl you gonna take off the tape so she can drink some water, but if she yells, the tape goes back on and a slap goes with it."

As soon as Rigo peels the tape off, the girl whispers, "You know who I am?"

"We don't care," Rigo whispers back. "Just drink, and you better keep quiet."

110

"I'm Rodriguez's daughter."

I was not expecting that. Feels like a bullet to the gut. This hurts.

"Yeah, his daughter, you fucking idiots!"

Just like that, we got played again. That's why Toño's tio is El Maistro. Fucking played.

"We thought you were his squeeze?" Rigo is more confused than I've ever seen him. And I've seen him so stoned he couldn't find the front door to the house at noon on a Sunday.

Jay looks so pissed, like he could blow us all up with one of those grenades.

"What? His girl? His hija?"

"I go to UT. I'm just here for break, motherfuckers."

"So, you're not his girlfriend? Really?" Rigo is winding his ass and scratching his watch, he's so confused.

"She said she's the daughter, Rigo." Fuck. I can't believe I had to fucking announce I would be in charge. Where the fuck is Toño?

"Girlfriend?" El Commandante's daughter scoffs. "My dad is gay, moron."

"Jay, we got the wrong girl."

"Yeah, I'm gathering that. So El Commandante is gay?"

"Jay, we got his daughter. This changes everything, I think."

"Ya think?" Jay looks like he's ready to punch Rigo, but he's also mystified. "So El Commandante is really fucking gay?"

"Do I need to spell it out for you fuckfaces? He's a genuine homo and has been for years—"

I step in as the new jefe. "Rigo, this don't change shit. We do our thing, like Toño planned."

"Whachalle! Jay, you think this changes anything?" Rigo is wound right up.

"No way, Rigo. We do it Toño's way, just that now we have more trading power. And most important, El Commandante is gay," Jays says through a giant smile.

As the new leader, I ask her name.

"Loraine. My name is Loraine, you fucker!"

"Orale, *Loraine*. Bit of a fucked up name for a Mexican chick, but okay." I'm all focus, deep breathing and everything. Good thing I got my yoga in. "Loraine, we are going to take you to your papi, but you have to go with us across the border, lay low, and meet him tomorrow. Entiendes."

"Why do I have to go across? I have to be in class in two days. And I have cheerleader tryouts...even though my dad said I've already made the team."

Jay says, "I bet he had to pay some money to get you a slot on the UT cheerleader's squad."

"No, I'm just that good, fool!"

"I ain't no fool, but whatever, Loraine. You have to do this with us, so get your mind right."

Jay has a flair for talking with this crazy chick, I must say.

"Okay, just don't tape me up anymore. I won't yell or try to get away."

We all take a sec, just to see....

"I said I won't try anything, you pussy mother—"

"Right." I tape Loraine's mouth as she continues cussing in murmurs.

"Tick tock, tick tock—three minutes to go, and no Toño," Rigo says.

I'm sweating. "We can't leave Toño. It's just not right."

"Jay, what do you think? I'm a soldier, and we leave in two. Ya vasta, Paco!"

The two minutes fly by, tis tas. "We are gone, bros. I'll drive the neighborhood streets, and that boat better be waiting for us in Zapata Viejo." Jay peels out like we're already being chased.

"Slow down, Jay!"

"Rigo, we got to move."

"You almost hit that ice cream truck, dude."

"We have to make the water. You know Mexico's guys are looking for us, and he who finds us gets paid. Every street in Monterrey has eyes, but we have speed on our side, so I'm fucking driving this piece of shit like a new fish in prison."

Rigo yells back, "Dale shine, ese! Let's just do it."

As we hit the dirt road out of Monterrey, everything goes from green to dead—the trees, even the cactus, don't grow out here. Dust everywhere, and not a car or bus in sight. Four miles to the river and this road sucks. The van better hold up.

"Oh boy, that a cop car up ahead? Rigo, you get in front with Jay. Lay your guns on your laps. Pronto."

Rigo gives me the "are your balls in your brain?" look.

"I said pronto. When you pull up to where they're blocking the road, just be cool. Smile and be nice."

"Paco, the crew boss! Orale."

"That's the spirit. Now calm your ass down and get in character. Let's make it past these cops. Stay frosty."

"Let's just do it."

"Let him see the guns, and we'll be okay."

"Okay," Jay stammers, "but if he makes a move, I'll kill him."

"Damn right, you will, Jay. And Rigo, you get the second cop. If he moves behind the van, I'll pop him. If I miss him, Jay, you take him. If he runs right, Rigo, he is yours."

"My left? Or your left, my right?"

"If he goes to your side, pop him, chingado! Pull up nice and smile at the jura."

The van stops. The fat cop on the driver's side waddles on over. "Papeles!"

Jay gives him Tex-Mex slang. "No gody papeles, osifer."

The cop yells, "¿Como que no?" He looks into the van and sees the pistols on Rigo and Jay's laps.

Jay and Rigo, both still smiling, wave.

The fat cop must be married with kids, because the look on his face says *these two guys smiling so sweet are going to kill me.*

The cop looks at Jay and smiles back. Then, with a laugh, he waves us on and keeps waving at us until we're out of sight. He knows if he makes a move, we will turn around and dust his ass.

I had a feeling they would let us go. Those cops are looking for travelers to shakedown; they can't do that if they're dead. Think about it—city cops outside the city limits. They probably aren't even on the clock, just freelancing to make ends meet. They're lucky we had places to go or we would be robbing them.

"Well, it worked. What a rush!"

"There's the turnoff to the river. Okay, Jay, get ready for anything. The boat guy might have snitched us off, or they pushed Toño hard to give up our exit. Either way, it's our only play."

The chica—Loraine—is surprisingly quiet. Rigo is scanning everything, good man. Jay's all focus. I don't' see anything. Looks clear. Might be one of those too good to be true situations, but I can practically hear the moisture in the air—it's that dead around here.

"We made it, Jay. You and Rigo look for the boat, and I'll stay with UT."

They get out and go to the shoreline for a better view. The Rio Grande looks the same from both sides of the bank, but it sure doesn't feel the same. I can see freedom from this side. It's just across the water—so close and so far away. Standing on this hot mesquite and cactus Mexican bank, I feel the weight of a lifetime of hurt. I can hear ghosts whispering in the wind. They're crying. They see freedom, too, but can't touch it. It's torture. Some places hold onto their history like a bad smell.

"Paco, I don't see any boat. No fucking boat!" Rigo yells. He's breathing heavy, sweating. He needs to calm down. This is not cool.

Think. I need to think.

Just then, here comes a bass tracker boat with twin 150 motors driving toward us, near the bank. As the boat gets closer, Rigo waves and jumps up and down at the driver. He looks like one of those blow-up dolls waving at customers off the freeway for "buy one get one free" pizza slices. I wanna tell him to settle his tan ass down, but the aluminum boat is sitting high on the water, letting us know nobody is hiding in there. This spells "go" to me.

I see Jay and Rigo talking to the boat guy and hugs all around. Who is that guy? Looks like…. No way. It's pinche Mike, our high school buddy. Holy shit, it's Mike. How the hell did Toño get Mike to stick his neck out? Mike don't do nothing for nobody, and nobody fucks with Mike—mainly because of his brother-in-law, but that's another story and I'm not Toño. That guy could come up with a story about shoelaces. Except all he does is work; I don't know where he finds the time to get so many stories. Anyway....

Rigo is walking back. He laughs as he opens the door. "It's pinche Mike, dude. You feel better?"

"UT, I'm cutting you loose," I tell Loraine. "Be cool."

I remove the tape and move aside so Rigo can finish.

She starts in, "Yeah, you guys are not going to get me in that shitty little boat."

Rigo laces into her. "It's the best we could get for your royal ass, so get up, UT, or I'll drag your cheerleading, jumping and yelling ass all the way to the boat."

"Cut her loose and carry her if you have to. Don't drag her, though, because we don't want marks unless totally necessary."

"Damn, Paco, I was just kidding. Besides, the dirt is soft and the water is nice and cool. She could use a dunk to cool her pissed off ass."

We load up in Mike's boat. UT has that look like she wants to bail out into the water and make a break to freedom.

"UT, you ever seen an alligator gar before?"

"No, whoever you are."

"I'm Paco. Alligator gars look savage like a gator, big-ass teeth, but have fins in place of those tiny legs. They're fast and they're all over this part of the lake. Keep your feet and hands in the boat. No funny business. Those princess fingers will make for a nice snack."

"I'm not scared!" she barks.

But she lost that look of wanting to run, which is what I wanted.

Mike takes us across the river to the US side. It takes all of fifteen minutes. Then he goes into the first cove and ties up.

"Mike, how you been? I never see you anymore." I wait till now to strike up a conversation. God knows why. Nerves, I guess.

"You cost us the game against United High School."

"That was years ago. Let it go, vato."

"I'm just saying, you did."

All of us are laughing, shaking the fear off our bones for a second. Except UT—she is motherfucking us under the tape.

"Mike, I'm taking the lead on this fiasco. We have to hold up somewhere unknown to anybody till eleven tomorrow. You got a place?"

"Toño called me and said he needed my help. Now, he doesn't call unless it's the real deal. He ran it down, and, well, he was my catcher on the baseball team and my best friend. And he gave me a number. I couldn't refuse."

"How much?"

"Rigo, it wasn't money, bro. Why is it always about the money? There's more to life. He gave me a phone number to a chick I liked back in high school. She just got divorced. Toño is hooking me up, ese."

Pinche Mike is glowing. Shit.

"You telling me he's not paying you for this piece of work?" I say.

"Damn right he is—ten Gs. But the digits are what sealed the deal. Now, this guy that owns this ranch—you know, El Sambo? He will let us use the place. I paid him, so we have the house to ourselves."

"Wasn't El Sambo the high school fuckup?"

"Yeah, Rigo, that's him. The world needs ditch diggers, too, you know."

As we jump out of the boat, we see only one truck parked by the dock.

"Dude, you have a truck, Mikey?"

"Yeah, a four-wheel drive."

"I know, but we are five bodies. Where we going to put the princess?"

"In the rear with the gear. Now, let's go."

We load up, and we off to the ranch house we go. It's only a mile way. I let UT suffer it out back with the gear, just to keep it real.

The evening is hot and quiet. No birds, no oilfields rocking, which means no tool pushers driving around. We see the ranch house, all sealed up, no cars in sight.

We pull up nice and slow. Rigo and Jay weapon up and clear the area and the house. I remove the tape from UT's mouth. She is quiet as a mouse, which makes me nervous. She's up to something.

"Don't do it."

"Do what, jerkoff?"

"Just don't do it. We'll have you home tomorrow. Just be cool."

"Prick, my dad is going to kill your sorry ass and feed you to the pigs."

"Get out of the truck and get inside the house before I clock you one, Loraine!"

Mike pulls up and takes his cap off, as if he's giving the okay to somebody. I never saw Rigo move behind cover so fast in my life.

Jay's gun is steadied on that space above Mike's eyebrows. "What you doing, bro? You setting us up?"

Shit. This is my team. Itchy fingers, greasy from sweat. Nervous. Shit.

Mike cracks a smile, looks over the hill. We see a dude walking toward us. He's got a long rifle over his right shoulder, like you would hold a sport coat.

"Dude, is that Jack? Fuck yeah, it is. I thought he was still in Huntsville's Walls Unit?"

Mike gives us a look. "Yeah, he's still in Huntsville, dumbass!"

Rigo pops up from his cover and starts to smile when he sees Jack. Jay is just posing with an "I'm Jay, you putos" look for all to see.

Jack sure is a sight for sore eyes. This dude is as bad as you can hire. And he's as good a shot with that .308 as any Marine sniper. Wait, he was a Marine sniper—one of the best. It is said he hit a guy with a .50 cal. from a mile away. More than once, this was rumored to have happened. He had some issues with authority and broke his commander's jaw over a card game; hence, several years in the brig. He came out, and it wasn't a month before he beat a guy into a coma and was shipped away to Huntsville Prison. Yeah, not a guy to cross. His nickname was "Coma Jack," cause there wasn't a guy he ever fought that didn't end up in a coma.

Jack walks up to the truck and gets in the passenger side without saying a word. He's got that thousand-yard stare, like a dude who's been in solitary for one too many days.

"Jack, it's me, Rigo. What's up, man?"

Jack looks at Rigo like he just walked over his grave, then stops himself. "Oh, man, it is you, Rigo. What the hell you doing here?"

"Jack, I'm in a shitstorm. Just trying to survive the day, my friend."

"Hey, Rigo, you still dating my sister?"

"No man, she married a dude from Hebbronville and has a kid now. Jack, how long were you gone, man?"

"Too fucking long. And as soon as I get out, I'm pushed to work for Toño's uncle on a debt I owed him from before I went in."

"When did you work for Toño's tio?"

"Who do you think had Paco on the scope when he was at the meet at El Mesquite?"

"That was you?"

"Yeah, I even waved at him."

"Oh, he said he saw a glass shine when he was out there."

"Next time, tell him not to wear jeans when everything is so dry. He stuck out like a watermelon in a cantaloupe patch."

Jack yells to Mike to get going because he has shit to do. Mike says his goodbyes and tells me he'll be back tomorrow at eleven. He jumps into the truck and smiles. "Get the fuck away from the truck, or I'll run your ass over."

And he would, too—he drives like shit. He once drove Toño's International Scout into the lake. Said it was in his blind spot.

I didn't ask them about that because, well, what's the use? Mike is a true pro. He drives off real slow as not to kick up dust that can be seen by neighbors, boats, and planes. I have to say, we're fucking lucky to have proper villains on this hunt.

The ranch house was typical of your South Texas-style shack. They all have all the deer antlers hanging in the kitchen, which is the main room where all the partying and drinking happens. The bedrooms are all in one, with a row of old beds collected from family and friends. They all have old coffee tin cans next to them, too, so if you have to go, all you have to do is pull it out and piss in the can. It beats having to walk to the outhouse with the snakes and spiders and shit. I can still hear the sound of piss hitting the can to this day.

We're all beat, but only hope to get an hour or two of sleep tonight. Can't help thinking they have our number and are moving for the kill as we sit here waiting for a miracle to occur tomorrow. The crew settles down in each corner of the shack, with UT sitting in a chair in the middle of the room. She's really quiet, until she lets out a scream and begins to motherfuck us all for taking her away from a party she was supposed to be at.

"You motherfuckers. I hate your asses. Just wait till my daddy gets ahold of you. He is going to rip your nuts off, pinche putos."

Jay stands up, and with the best vato voice, he says, "Hey, esa, you eat with that mouth?"

"Fuck you, you Danny Trejo wannabe!"

Rigo pipes in, "I told you, dude, you really look like him!"

Jay wants to be pissed, but he's holding back a smile. "Who you callin' Danny Trejo?"

I put a hand over her mouth and whisper, "Shh. You're going home tomorrow, so let's make the best of it and just hang in there for a bit longer, okay?"

Toño always said to keep the scared rabbit happy. I get it now—keeping UT comfortable and safe will only help us in the long run. My new job is to make sure we get her to the Mesquite tomorrow, unharmed.

All I could tell her was that it was a job and we were delivering her to her mama tomorrow—safe and sound. And to get ready to cheer for the Longhorns.

UT says, "Wait, my mom?"

"Oh, I'm sorry. No, your happy-ass daddy!"

"Oh hell, I'm telling my dad you were making fun of him being gay, you bastard."

"I'm just kidding, UT. Lighten up."

We all got a big laugh, except UT. I would love to see her walking down Sixth Street in Austin; I bet she's a complete bitch to everyone. You have to like a girl like that.

Everything eventually relaxes and slows down to a crawl. It is quiet here at the ranch. All you can hear is the wind whisking between the mesquites as the moon lights up the darkness. The night is cool, around seventy-five degrees. That's one thing that is the best in South Texas—the cool badass nights. Everything else sucks in these South Texas towns, but the nights are groovy.

I know we're all wondering what happened to Toño. Is he dead or alive? Toño has put some big noise into this job that none of us could have seen coming. The big swing, the shift to Monterrey. And how the hell did he get Mike and Jack to join the crew? None of us could ever pull this off without getting killed just for trying. I hope Toño is on his way from Mexico and will be there waiting for us at the meet. It's hard going blind to a deal where you know you might not get out alive. But tonight—no booze, mota, or sleep. We just have to get the deal done and let the chips fall where they may.

Damn, I hate taking over the crew on this deer hunt. Toño knew I would jump in as jefe if he had to disappear. He had to have known it might turn out this way.

I remember the first run we ever made together, just the two of us. We were in high school, and he comes by my house in his old International Scout. All he said was, "Paco, let's go get a six-pack." Next thing I know, we're hauling ass out of Rio Grande City with fifty pounds of weed and two Star County deputies on our asses. All Toño kept saying was, "Paco, keep looking for the county line." Well, I'm just glad I helped him hot rod that Scout in auto mechanic's shop our freshman year, or we would have been dragged and tagged by those fucking Rio Grande deputy puto's. As we crossed the Star County/Zapata County line, those deputies didn't dare cross into Zapata with us. They would have never made it back home, and they knew it. Toño looked at me, and I still remember his words: *"Paco—this game of smugglers you can play, but it is up to you and you alone, homes, to learn it right."*

I thought he was just bullshitting me, but today it makes a lot of sense. I know the game; I just have to put foot to ass and get us all the way home.

That Toño is a smart motherfucker. I have to start thinking like him, and his uncle. I have to see five moves ahead. But that Toño didn't give me all the pieces. I have to trust he put me here for a reason, and he knows how I do things—"Give it a name."

The sun starts to break, and reality starts to hit Rigo and me—this might be the last sunrise our eyes see. Jay is dead to the world, snoring like a busted chainsaw. Rigo goes outside to see a man about a horse. I move to the corner of the kitchen, staring at bigmouthed UT, thanking God I'm still alive, which means I have a fighting chance. Look at this shit—Loraine is leaned over the table. She's drooling all over, and she's still good-looking. This chick is hot, with a Tex-Mex look to her. They say NY chicks are tough; let them come down to the border. These chicks here have been taught to shoot, fight, and fuck their way out of anything. Oh, can you picture a catfight with UT and a tough NY Italian girl? Oh yeah—my lifesavings would be on UT.

Rigo comes in and wakes up Jay. He makes a sound like a bell in prison. Jay shoots up like a rattler bit him on the ass, yelling, "Ready, ready!"

Pinche Rigo laughs.

"What the fuck, Rigo? I thought I was back in the can."

Rigo keeps chuckling as Jay sweats it out and shakes it off. He then wakes her majesty for no real reason but to fuck with her.

"Let's see what we have for breakfast in this shithole," I suggest.

"Yes, boss. Anything you say, boss!" Rigo is taking this jefe thing too far.

All we have is a can of refried beans and tortillas. Fuck it, Jay, bean tacos all around. There's nothing like having a belly of gas to pass the time of day with friends.

We get the tacos rolling. UT wants cheese, lettuce, and some pico de gallo for hers. Jay slides her some hot sauce and old jalapeños that were sitting in a jar for God knows how long. That bitch has had enough of this shit. She starts to make a break for the door, then stops, turns around, and sits back down when she sees not one of us has moved or pulled a piece. She's not as dumb as she looks. She's safer in here than she is out there.

"No, I'm not running off," she snaps. "I want to see your stupid faces when my dad beats your ass."

Jay, with the calmest voice, says, "So you want the jal-apeños, baby?"

With the nicest smile, UT turns to Jay and whispers, "Don't you ever call me baby, or I will take those jalapeños and shove them where the sun don't shine, jerkoff."

She really doesn't like being called "baby."

After the banquet, everyone's quiet. Probably thinking about what we might have to leave behind; I know I am. The families that have worked all their lives to make this harsh territory a better place for us. Our friends that we grew up with and the stories we have between each other. When you grow up in a town with a population that rides around 3K, you absolutely know everybody. The kind of person they are—from the town child molester we tor-mented on a weekly basis to the DPS officer we all re-spected and left alone to live out his retirement. How bad do you have to screw the pooch to end up here in Zapata, Texas? But the fiber of our people is strong and their word is their bond. Without character, you are neither a man nor are you respected. Shit, even the crooks follow the rules of our community. Leaving this all behind is hard, but breathing is a fair tradeoff.

We will learn to live with the rest.

The sun rises quickly, it seems. Jay shouts, "Everybody take all the ammo out of your guns and reload."

UT, with that smartass tone, whines, "Why on earth would you take the ammo out just to put it back in?"

"We can't get into a gunfight, princess, without knowing how many rounds we have. Gotta be prepared for a run and gun."

Look at that...why would Rigo tell her about a possible firefight?

"Gunfight? Gunfight? You never said anything about a gunfight! I'm supposed to be delivered to my dad in one piece, that's what you said. Remember?"

Rigo looks right through her. "I have fifty-two rounds in three mags for my Glock."

That shuts her up fast, but you can see the "oh shit" look on her face. She is worried.

Being the new Ram Rod, I jump in. "UT, your pop won't put you in the position. You'll be home by lunchtime, going back to whatever it is you do and getting ready for college. You will be fine. I give you my word."

"You're Paco, right?"

"Yes, I am. A tu servicio."

"Well, Paco, take that broom over there and shove it right up your ass. I am not scared."

That's better. Stay tough, girl. I got her back in the right mindset.

Jay pops up. "I have six for the revolver, and one seventeen-round mag for my Glock."

Rigo hands Jay one of his Glock mags.

"Paco, what do you have on you?"

129

"I have fifty-two rounds with my Glock. If it gets hot, I can toss you guys one of my mags. Remember, we're going to the entrance of El Mesquite Ranch. Hopefully, Mexico and El Commandante and his men will be waiting for us. If we have to wait for them, we'll give them thirty minutes before we bail."

Jay asks, "What about the girl?"

"We drop her off there and we split to you-know-where."

UT asks, "Where you going that my dad won't find your stupid asses?"

Rigo looks at me. "Tell her a story."

Jay says, "A story? I want to hear a story. Like in the yard when I was in the can and I was bored."

"Okay, boys. UT, I am going to pass on some wisdom I was given by an old vato back home, so listen up. This vato is 101 years old, and was a badass back in the day. It's said he even road with Villa. Well, I asked him what the secret of living a long life was. And do you know what he said? Well, of course you don't, UT. I have boots older and smarter than you."

Rigo, Jay, and UT are pulled into the story like a fat man to a taco truck.

"He says to me, '*Mijo, the secret to living long is...mind your own fucking business.*'"

All three start the cursing at me. "Man, fuck you!"

"You sucked us in, you fucker!"

"So, you don't need to know, *Lorraine!*"

"My dad is going to beat your asses. Just wait."

After everything settles down, Rigo asks, again, about Toño.

"Toño is either going to be at the meet, or he's gone." This is the fourth time I've answered that. "What do you think, Jay?"

"That vato has ten lives, and I know he is still around. He wouldn't fuck us. If he had, we would have been hit at the river with pinche Mike."

Jay's answer beats mine.

Rigo smiles. "Yeah, you're right. Toño does have the head to be the Big Noise in the Valley. I hope to see him again. I also think they won't kill an earner like him. That would be stupid."

I look at the guys. I'm worried. "Get ready, cause Mike will be here to pick us up soon. Vatos. Abrasos. We are going to do this with big balls, and fuck those putos. This is our town. Let's show them how we do it Valley-style. Rigo, get UT cleaned up and ready to go meet her papa."

UT gets up and starts again. "You guys ain't tough enough to deal with my dad. You're fucked!"

I've had enough. "UT, you want the tape back on?"

"Paco, you're the boss, joto!"

"Shut that cheerleader mouth and save it for Sixth Street. And when you do get your ass to Austin, I want you to go to the Dirty Dog Saloon and tell the owner, Shitty, to buy you a beer on me. Then ask him who we really are, Loraine. We are proper villains."

15

THE RUN

We see Mike coming by, the dust flying in the cendero. A car is following him.

Shit!

"UT, lie down by the fireplace in case the bullets start flying. Lay down, UT, for your own good! Jay, take left flank, and, yes, my left, and try to cover the rear. Rigo, take the right window and cover me, I'll go out to meet them."

By the time I'm out the door, one, two, three, Mike is on top of us. He's parking.

As he approaches, I draw my Glock. "Mike, stop!"

As I draw a bead on his head, pinche Mike starts laughing. "It's Jack. He's driving the other car, you dumbass."

I wanted to hug him right there, but I know they would have cut or stabbed me on principle. Mean bastards. El Machete wouldn't even mess with Jack. If Jack walked in a bar, Machete would leave. Jack's a tall bastard and lean, like a goddamned Olympic swimmer, except Mexican. It creates a strange image in my mind every time I think of it, but he's skinny like that—like his skin has been shrink-wrapped around his muscles. Michael fucking Phelps; I am not joking. But when he stands up he looks like a giant. As mean as El Machete is, he knows who not to mess with. Jack is at the top of that list. The wind is shifting in our direction. I can feel it. Badass Jack is our ante, and we just upped it by six-foot-three.

"Come in, guys."

"No, we're leaving. Here's your car for the meet," Mike says, handing me the keys.

"Jack, you bring your rifle?"

"Well, Toño also put me on his payroll for the action, so yes, I have my .308. And I'll be covering you guys when you make the break to the Gata Orcada Ranch and head to the river. Anybody follows you, I go to work." Then Jack looks right into me and adds, "Next time we come to help your asses, don't have your boys pointing guns at us, or I will cut you all down and leave you for crow bait. You got that?"

"You know the game. We didn't know who was with Mike in the second vehicle. Toño taught me not to take any chances. You of all people know that."

Mike grunts. "Jack they're doing the same thing we would do. Let it go. It's Paco, man. He's one of us, bro."

With that, Mike jumps in the truck with Jack, and they drive off without another word. As I watch them go, I feel clammy all over, like I just got out of my worst confession with only a dozen Hail Marys on my back. Not bad.

I can't wait to tell the guys about our guardian angel. As I walk back to the shack, I'm high-stepping it like a polka dance.

Jay immediately yells, "What?"

"We have our car for the meet, and Toño got Jack on the payroll. He's our fucking cover, baby!"

"No fucking way! Toño had them both on the payroll before we even went to do the drag?"

"Feel better, boys. We're going to do this. Let's give them an hour to go get set, and then we go."

Jay, being the old pachuco, goes, "Let's not start sucking each other's dicks just yet. We still have a ways to go."

I get back in character and order Rigo to go check the car and make sure it's all running right. And I tell him to sweep it for trackers and shit. Then I inform UT we have an hour. She can relax. I even apologize for the scare. I'm that happy.

"Fuck you, whoever you are," she responds.

"Again, my name is Paco, Lorraine! Are you simple, girl?"

"Whatever, Paco!"

"I fucking hate that 'whatever,' UT. If you were my daughter, I'd have that mouth of yours permanently taped, entiendes! How the hell does Light-loafers Daddy put up with you?"

"He puts up with me just—"

"It was a rhetorical question, Loraine. You know what those are? That means I just gave you something to think about while you keep your mouth shut."

Rigo gives me a strange look.

"What? You think Toño's the only one who knows big words? I went to grammar school, too, my brother."

You should see Rigo's face. He's got nothing. It's not his fault; this is the most he's heard me talk since we actually were in grammar school.

"We have to start going over the route we need to take to San Ygnacio." Jay's all ears when I say this. "We have to come out of this ranch, and if that part is safe, then we have fifteen miles to drive before we get to El Mesquite just before San Ygnacio. Driving through Zapata is more of a roll of the dice—we have to go through the backroads. But because Zapata is so small, we'll be seen by anyone that's looking for us. There are eyes in those hills. Then, getting on Highway 83 to the meet is just suicide. The highway is a piranha pit, two lanes of open freeway that screams death at every turn. You just can't protect yourself in an open road like that. It's built for ambushes and traps. If they're planning to hit us, it will be on those roads."

Man, Toño is the master planner for this type of shit. He was taught by the best, by his tio—planned everything with three different routes and escapes.

Jay says. "We have the girl—they have to be scared about hitting her, don't they?"

"Yeah, but roadblocks, spikes on the road...anything could happen."

Rigo comes back with a note he found taped to the visor of our new ride. "Paco, Toño left us another note. Read it, boss."

"Enough with that 'boss' shit, Rigo. It's getting old, brother. Let's step outside where UT can't hear. Jay, keep an eye on her from the window."

We all go. I read the note:

"Boys, go north toward Hebbronville. Two miles up take a left at Panchitos Ranch. Go all the way north through the ranch roads all the way to La Perla Ranch. Turn left through La Perla's back gate then hit Highway 83. From there, it's only two blocks from the meet. All the ranchers have unlocked and opened the gates. If Jay is driving, you'll be on time.

Good Luck,

Toño."

"Fuck me, Jay, you heard the man. We go toward Hebbronville...."

"Shit, we'll be about fifteen minutes late going that way."

"Shut up, Rigo it ain't no thing!"

"But we'll get there alive," Jay says.

"Two miles north and fifteen across ranch roads." I study my men. They look ready to shift gears. "Boys, we're going to make this play. Pinche Toño has to be alive."

"Why you say that, Paco?"

"Faith, putos."

"Rigo, go inside and tape UT's mouth and hands only, and load her up. We are leaving now."

Rigo walks up to UT with the tape behind his back. By the time she spots it, all that comes out of her trap is a tiny murmur. Nice. I needed that small break.

"Yeah, shut up, Loraine!" Rigo says with a smile.

"Let's go. We probably will make it by 12:15, so let's hit the road, Jay."

It's hot as sin, and everything from the ranch to the highway is dead; not even the cactus want to live in this heat. I pray we can get to the cutoff in Hebbronville without being seen by all the eyes wanting to collect a paycheck.

As we creep along through Zapata, I start to remember places where my friends live, where Toño and I played basketball at the Lions Club. We road our bikes all over this town. I remember when we were kids, a guy named To-masito Pio Pio used to ride around on his bike. Tomasito Pio Pio was touched (as they called it)—a forty-year-old man with a ten-year-old mind. He used to wear tight blue jeans with shiny black dress shoes, and he always had his curly hair parted to one side. I swear he looked just like Kramer from *Seinfeld*. He always had a box in the basket on the front of his bike. He would pull up to us, and Toño always asked Tomasito Pio Pio, "Who is the baddest guy in town?" Tomasito would set his kickstand, open up the box, and pull out a baby chick. Then he'd hold it by his face and ask the chick in a loud voice, "Who is the baddest guy in town?" Tomasito would squeeze the chick and you would hear the chick yelp—*pio pio pio!* Tomasito would then glare at us, nod his head, and whisper, "Pio Pio." Those were the days I will never forget.

It really stings that we have to be hunted like dogs when this is our town and our people. Who are these guys to run our lives like cattle? Buying and selling us by the pound, and then discarding us like trash without a thought. This shit has to change, or South Texas will be doomed and abandoned by the very folks that started this town when the dam was built over a hundred years back.

Toño and I talked about shifting the power, using the money to go legit. What are they going to do if you buy businesses and land? Toño always said get your ducks in order, and when the hammer falls and the cartels and dope dries up, we can still get out. But we have to survive to live a different life. Might be a dream, but it's something.

Taking all the backroads has given us an edge on those out-of-towners, so I'm a little more relaxed in that regard. We finally hit the road to Hebbronville.

"Jay, drive it like you stole it from an ex-girlfriend, but without wrapping it around a tree," I say.

Jay guns it just the right amount.

Two miles up, we see Panchito's Ranch. The gate is wide open, just like Toño promised. This is never done, because the cows and horses get out and thieves get easy access. That's what's so surreal about it. Jay zips through like it's his ranch. I don't know who the hell will be closing those gates, and I don't look back to find out.

We make the turn toward San Ygnacio. The fucking roads are really bad, ruts everywhere up and down. We go, but we're making good time only if this car holds up. I wish we had a four-wheel drive rather than this piece of shit— 1980 Galaxy 500 like Burt Reynolds in *Gator*. I can't even believe this car still exists. I know who used to own it, and he drove the shit out of it.

Driving on ranch roads, you can really see the raw beauty of South Texas. It's hard land, but if you know what to look for, you can see where the ponds feed the animals, and where the ranchers burn cactus to feed the cows. There are salt licks everywhere. And some of these ranch houses have been here since before Texas took it over.

They don't even look real; they look like they were built for a movie set. I'll miss the BBQs and pachangas (parties) with the guys, riding horses and getting full of beer and fajitas.

"Okay, Jay, here comes La Perla Ranch. Take a hard left, and that will take us to the highway. What the—!" The gate is closed and locked. No way.

"Rigo, get out there and shoot that lock off," Jay orders.

"No, we can't shoot the lock. We are about a half-mile from the meet. They'll hear the shot."

"What do we do, Paco?"

I can hear Rigo sweating, I swear.

Just about then, we see an old, red Ford Super cab pull out of La Perla Ranch, heading toward the gate. And then an old dude—I think it's Old Man Jasso, no shit. He gets out and unlocks the gate for us. Then he holds it open so it won't swing back and hit our car. We can't believe this shit, and drive up to thank him.

"Can't leave my gate open. The cows get—"

"—Will get out." I grin.

Old Man Jasso tips his hat. I pretend to do it back, seeing as how I ain't wearing one.

Jay drives us through.

Rigo yells out the window, "Thank you, Mr. Jasso. Say hello to your daughter for me."

Jasso yells back a string of fuck yous, adding, "Leave my daughter alone, pinche puto!"

Old man Jasso caught Rigo in his house with his daughter bent over South Texas-style.

"Rigo, what is your fucking problem? You got refried beans for brains. The guy might've just saved our lives."

"I was just saying hi. I thought he was over it."

Jay starts laughing. "A father doesn't get over that, dumbass."

"Shut up, Trejo."

Jay cannot seem to stop laughing. "Was she good?"

"Guys, let's get on point here. We're almost at the highway."

We can see the entrance to El Mesquite.

"Jay, drive up cool, like you're leaving the bar at 2:00 a.m."

Jay drives up smooth. At the same time, we pull out our guns and get ready for anything. Really, it could be anything.

16

THE LAST STAND

We roll up and over the hill to the entrance. Three black Suburbans are blocking the road. I quietly ask Rigo to take the tape off UT's mouth and hands. "Stop short, Jay, and I'll walk up. You guys keep a gun on UT and stay low. If I get cut down, back out and make the run like we planned."

"No way, Paco," Rigo whispers, "We're in for a penny, in for a pound, ese."

"No. Just go and make the boat."

Just about then, two trucks pull up behind the car.

"Well, we are trapped, boys," Jay declares.

"Let's play this out," I advise. As I walk out of the car, I leave my gun with Jay. He'll need it more than I will.

I start my walk up to the shiny, newest Suburban, the one with the cool back windows Chevy had redesigned for the new models. Looks badass. I get about ten yards shy, and eight guys bail out with submachineguns—all MP5s, which usually means mercs. I raise my arms and turn nice-n-easy to show them I'm unarmed. They grab me and pat me down like you would a stripper leaving your house at 3:00 a.m. They bind my hands behind my back with zip ties. I look back and see four guys bail out of trucks behind our car. Of all people, Big Head is with them. How could you miss that big water head? The back left window of the middle Suburban rolls down. Inside, and I can see an old Mexican dude—Mexico, in a sweet, shiny silver sharkskin suit. Next to him is El Commandante in his uniform. I guess he thinks if he gets caught in Texas, it might help him get released or something.

I keep telling myself what Toño beat into me when dealing with these cats: Don't say shit.

Mexico shouts, "You're late, pendejo! Where is the girl?"

This guy speaks good English. Probably educated in the states.

"We are delivering her to you, sir. She is in the car. Unharmed."

Mexico nods, then screams, "Bring her here, now!"

"You want me to go get her or have my boy bring her?" It's an honest question from a guy without a weapon, whose hands are zip-tied behind him. This is worse than being handcuffed.

"You fucking idiot! Have her here now!"

I look at the car and head wave Rigo to bring the girl up. Rigo gets out with UT. As soon as her feet hit the ground, she runs up to the Suburban. Rigo freezes and slowly starts backing up to the car. The guys in the trucks surround our vehicle. Rigo just stops and gives up. He is fucked in the wind.

UT runs to her dad's side. He opens the door and hugs her. She begins to motherfuck us about how we taped her mouth and hands. Her dad just keeps asking, "Are you hurt?" She won't shut up about how we're assholes and we made her eat cold beans with rotten jalapeños. Her dad again asks, "Did they touch you or anything like that?"

"They taped my mouth like four times, those dumbass motherfuckers! What else do you need to know? Stomp their asses! I missed a party and cheerleading!" Then she looks back at us and snarls, "Fuckers!"

Damn, she's loud.

The dad looks at Mexico with a bored nod. That nod speaks volumes—it says she's fine and a she's a spoiled bitch. Mexico gets it. Hell, I got it and I just met these fine fellows.

Mexico then turns and looks at me and with what appears to be a bothered glance. "Okay, putos, we have business to take care of, so get the hell out of here. There is only one reason you're still alive, so don't fuck it up."

The window goes up, and all I can see is my reflection now. Some of their guys come up behind me—I feel like I'm in a movie at this point, watching it all in the reflective glass. They spin me around and cut my hands loose. As I begin to walk away in a daze, this blond-haired bodyguard hands me a cold steel knife. I look at the weapon in my hand. Now I know they killed him. They killed Toño. I could fucking puke, and I do this shit for a living. I hold up Toño's knife and point it to the yellow hair and whisper, "You will see this knife again. I swear to you, you will see it again."

He smiles and walks away.

Just like that, they load up and drive away toward El Mesquite to finish with the treachery of Toño's uncle and that fat fuck Machete.

I stand in the dust bowl as they drive off. We're still alive. The Suburban with the major players and UT go in the direction of the highway, leaving the dirty work to the soldiers. Cowards.

I'm still for a second like the wind in July. Then, shit! I run to the car, nearly plowing over Rigo, who has been turned to stone or some shit. He's standing there like a damn deer in the headlights.

"Let's go, Rigo, let's go!"

By the grace of God, Rigo snaps out of it and dives into our wheels, just as Jay guns it.

"What happened? What just happened, homes?" Jay starts in.

"Just drive, Jay. Just get us to the river and let's make that boat. Mexico said one thing was keeping us alive? I have no idea what the hell that is, but I'll take it."

We hit the highway. "Go, Jay, go baby!" There's two miles to go till the turnoff.

I look back at Rigo. He's just sitting in the car with this blank look—worse than when he was drunk on mescal and couldn't find the front door of the casa. Totally blank.

"Rigo, you okay, ese? Rigo!"

"I'm okay. I just don't know, I, I...."

"Okay, yes, I got it. You're alive. We're all alive. It's surprising, to say the least. Now grab your gun. We have to make it to the river."

It's quiet again, like on the way in last night. Nobody even notices the metal in my hand—the knife. It keeps distracting me, that's for sure.

Jay yells, "We got a tail!"

A mile to go, and an older Suburban sneaks up behind us. It's coming up fast.

"Just go and make the turn. We have no idea what's waiting for us, and we're so close. Keep them off our ass, Jay. Earth to Rigo—you locked and loaded?"

"This piece of shit is giving me all she's got, vatos. That's it."

The Suburban is coming around our left side.

"Rigo, get ready!"

As they start pulling up left, we start our turn to the right.

"Wait!" I yell out with a weirdly girlish voice. "It's Pokey! It's Pokey. Don't shoot."

He blows by us, holding up a Lone Star beer can, flipping us off and laughing his ass off. Pokey is another school friend, going back home to Zapata after a stretch on a Rig. That fucking son of a bitch. He does have a hot rod Suburban, now that I recall, and it can haul ass. Didn't I say in a town of 3K you know absofuckinglutely everybody? Of all the days to be driving around like an asshole in a Suburban. I swear, Pokey has always had the worst timing. That's how he got tossed in the tank the first time. That's one fine story. Wish Toño was here to do what he does best—tell it.

We make the turn into the Gata Orcada Ranch. Half a mile to the river—easy, but we're on another bad dirt road.

"Jay, please don't fuck up the car before we get there. Please make it."

I got it. I'll swing around the tumbleweeds—won't tear up the oil pan or mufflers. Don't worry, my brother."

One hundred yards from the river, we can see a small dock, but....

"What the.... No boat? Where's Mike?"

"You don't think they dropped him, do you, Paco?"

"Mike? He's with Jack. What do you think, Rigo?"

We get to the dock. Still no Mike, and no boat to save our lives. We look at each other. We're pigs heading to the slaughter. We get out of the car. It's popping and smoking. In the distance, we can hear a motorboat coming around the bend toward the dock. It feels right. It's Mike. We all want to cry.

Rigo falls to his knees, because how much can a man take?

Jay, on the other hand, is in his pachuco stand, all leaned back and shit. He looks different from how he usually does, like he's daring you to say something stupid so he can shove his gun up your ass. Right now, he looks happy. And fearless. Like he had envisioned all of this.

Pinche Mike pulls up, laughing. "Que paso?"

All I can say is, "Dude, let's pack up and go."

We load up, but Mike won't leave. Looks like he's thinking about casting a line and pulling up a seat. What the fuck?

"Mike, let's go."

"Not until you guys dump your quetes in the drink right now."

"What the hell you saying, you crazy?" Jay's happy just got drained.

"Toño left orders not to take you guys until you dump your rods in the river, so dump them or you stay here."

Jay raises his gun. "Drive, or I'll make a canoe of your head."

I had to remind Jay to lower his gun or he is dead—Jack!

Jay thinks about it for a second, then drops the gun over the edge and into the river. Rigo and I look at each other and drop all the guns. We watch them sink to the bottom.

What the fuck are we doing?

Mike laughs and drags his hand across his chest. One hundred yards out, Jack stands up, holding his rifle across his chest and smiling. He didn't have to kill his friends—that's what that smile is all about. He would've killed us, but is glad he didn't.

Mike yells, "Now we can go."

Toño left instructions for the pickup. What the hell was he doing to us now? I got his metal tucked inside my drawers. No one said toss Toño's knife over. It's not a gun, in any case. We drive out to the river in the bass tracker. The waves are hard. We hold on for dear life as Mike opens up the outboard motors, the boat banging every wave from Texas to Mexico. Mike drives out toward El Tigere Island, and then back toward the Mexico side. We see an opening, and Mike pulls up to the bank. "Get out and walk over the hill."

Rigo asks, "What's over the hill?"

"I don't know. Toño didn't tell me. Get off my boat."

"I hope to see you again, Mike," I say. "I'll buy you some beers."

"You just might see me again. Now, get off my boat. I have to get home and watch *Wheel of Fortune*."

"Life goes on, doesn't it, Mike?"

"Dude, it always does, and the party never ends. Beat it."

Mike drives off and leaves us standing on a bank in Mexico with no money, no guns, no food, no drink, and no car. Oh, and let me add, with Mexican killers looking for us in every town on the border.

I get back in character. "Let's walk over the hill and see what's next."

"You want to split up? Take flank and—"

"No, Rigo. Let's just walk up the middle of the hill like we own it."

The hill is bare, just like everything around us. The sky is blue without a cloud, and you can see the heat bouncing off the ground. I bet I could cook an egg on the dirt, it's so hot. Tarzan couldn't live here.

Damn, we are dirty, smelly, and starving. It's times like this I wish they would just shoot us and get this shit over with. We hit the hill and Jay starts his pachuco walk.

"Jay, why do pachucos walk all falling back and shit?"

"Mira, boys, the pachuco walk is our way of identifying other pachucos from a distance. Sort of why black guys always grab their balls."

"Why do black guys always grab their balls, Jay?"

"Because that's the only thing the white people haven't taken from them!"

"Pinche, Jay, you said a joke!"

He is the man. Just ask him—he'll tell you. Rigo and I stroll like we don't have a care in the world.

17

THE TRIP

We're baking in the Mexico heat—100 degrees or more—no water, tequila, or beer...and here we are walking over this hill, having no idea what is waiting for us. We get to the top of the hill. There's the Ford LTD by the side of the road down below. Problem is, it's next to a Mexican cop car.

Jay yells, "Paco!"

"Yeah, I know. Fuck, I got eyes. Let's go get our car, and fuck those juras."

As we get close, two cops pile out. Motherfucker—it's the fat cop and his partner from Monterrey.

They wave and smile.

"You believe this shit, Rigo?"

"This ain't no coincidence, Jay. I think we might be okay."

"Hombres!" the fat cop yells out. "Su carro los espera."

I ask the fat cop, "Toño?"

"Por su puesto, arreglo todo." Then he says, "Vallan con dios!"

You too, fucker. We load up. Jay's driving, of course. The fat fuck cop is still waving at us until we get out of sight. What's up with that shit?

"Rigo, check the glove box and look for a note. I'll start praying."

"Nothing. Not a damn thing but fuses."

"Check the visor, Jay."

An envelope falls on Jay's lap—here's hoping our life-line is inside. I'd cry tears of joy, but I'm too tired.

As I take the envelope, I noticed there's a childish smile painted all over Jay's face—one I have never seen before. Comical. I start opening the envelope. Feels like Christmas morning.

"What does it say?"

"It says back off, puto. I'm kidding, bro. *If you're reading this, you're bad motherfuckers. You know where I left the money, I bet Rigo is back there looking for it. Rigo, use your knife.*" I hand Rigo the knife I've had strapped to my gut. "Here you go."

"What are you doing with Toño's knife?"

"One of Mexico's guys gave it to me."

Yeah, Rigo, to answer your next question: he's dead. I give him a very specific look, a "shut the fuck up and let's not talk about it" look.

Silence fills the car, but then Rigo ignores the gesture and asks the damn question anyway. "You think he still might...?"

Jay, with his coldest voice, jammers. "He's exed out. It's done."

Rigo pulls the seat up and cuts the back lining. A bundle of money wrapped in foil hits the floor. "Dude, this is a lot of cash."

Jay orders, "Read the letter, Paco. Where the fuck we going?"

"*Directions: Drive to Cancun and make sure you drive around the towns, not through them. Go south 90 miles to Tulum and bang a left to the resorts by the ocean. Don't stop and drink, Jay. Take a right and go all the way past the resorts to the Yucatan Reserve Arch. A guy will ask you your business. Ask for Pedro Infante, and, no, not the actor. That's his real name, Rigo.*"

"How did he know I was going to say that?"

"*Hand him 500 cash and he will let you into the reserve without signing in. One road, so go ten miles into the reserve and you will see a sign on your left, 'Rancho Pedro Paila,' take a left and pull up to the main house.*"

"What else does it say?" Rigo asks.

"Nothing else. So what do you guys want to do? Follow this map, or make our own run? Rigo?"

"I say trust Toño. He's had the lead on the horse this whole time. I say do it."

"Jay?"

"You know, this has been a hard, bad, fucked-up action. But I vote like a soldier following the leader. Let's go, hombres. What do you think, Paco?"

"What do I think? I think this is our best shot to stay alive."

We all yell out, "Orale!"

"Yucatan, baby. How bad could it be?"

"It's a two-day drive, guys, so let's hit it."

We only stop to gas up, piss, and pick up food. Not knowing what's ahead or what's waiting for us, on we go. Talk is small. We take turns driving and sleeping, or trying to sleep. Fear and heat have a crazy way of combining to keep a man up. The closer we get, the tighter my stomach gets. We drive through the shittiest neighborhoods of these Mexican towns. They look like warzones, and the people look beat down, like someone clobbered them on the head repeatedly with their own damn dreams, beating them till they can no longer spell the word *esperansa.*

We finally hit Tulum and bang a left toward the ocean. The drive from there to the shore is about five miles. The air is dirt dry, and it looks like every swinging dick is on a bicycle. You can tell there is money around here by the Exxon gas stations with the grocery stores that are about a half-acre long. Yeah, a lot of euro trash come here to rest and play. Tourists are everywhere. And the chicks—wow, wearing barely anything. It's beauty to behold, that's for sure.

Jay yells out to some European chicks with dreads and tanned bodies, "Chicas!" Then he makes a kissing sound, and we are every kind of bad cliché.

"Jay, like you know Europeans, mammon."

"Fuck you, Rigo, I'm getting tired of your shit."

"Jay, there's the Arch."

"What's that dudes name again?"

"Pedro Infante, stupid!"

"Rigo, I swear I'm gonna kick your ass."

"Pull up, Jay, here comes the Mayan-looking guard, so be cool."

The cop—or security dude—asks, "¿Que negocio?"

Jay says, "We want to talk to Pedro Infante."

The Mayan laughs. "The actor?"

His laughter stops when he notices our stares drilling through him.

He straightens up real fast. "Quinientos Americanos," he says, barely above a whisper.

I hand him 500 clams. He counts it, then waves us through.

"What next?"

"These guys might just kill us just to find out what else we have, so drive, Jay. Set the odometer to ten miles."

"Odometer? This piece of shit barely runs, nothing works. Odometer? You're lucky it came with an ignition."

"Just go. And keep an eye out for the sign Pedro Paila Ranch."

This road is the worst road anyone of us have ever seen, and we have seen some bad roads. The ruts are wide and deep, and we can't drive faster than ten miles an hour even if we wanted to.

Seems like we've been driving for hours, but we can see the ocean to our left, and that calms us down and gives us hope. Why? I have no idea, but right now, we'll take anything we can get.

Suddenly Rigo's on his toes, head out the window like a fucking Labrador. "Jay, on your left! You see the sign? We are here! We are here, we made it!"

We turn left through an open gate, start yelling and screaming like kids on a Six Flags coaster. But as we pull up to this beautiful, white, two-story house, that tight feeling in my gut hits me again.

"Pull up to the back door and let's play the hand, boys,"

Jay whispers, "Paco, are you sure this is the right place?"

Just about then, a guy wearing a white shirt and white pants stops at the back door. He stands at attention, smiling at us. We get out of this shit car, smelly and tired. It's around 3:00 p.m. Mexico time. It's hot, but the ocean breeze is cool to the skin.

The Mexican that's blanco'd out from head to toe states, "Señores, entren."

As we walk in to this beautiful house, two girls greet us. They point to all the items on the table.

The guy in white starts describing everything. "Tequila, vino, vodka, y Indio cervesa. Steaks, papas, frijoles, arros, guacamole, tortillas. Para ustedes."

"Paco." Rigo leans in. "Did he just say all this is for us?"

"Yes, he did. But don't ask why. Just let it be."

"He said he has our rooms ready with new duds."

"Maybe I like my old duds," Jay quips.

"I don't think so. Not a trace of Trejo is left in you, bro."

"You want to start with me, Rigo?"

Then Blanco says, "Bien provecho." And with that, he leaves the house.

Once Rigo shuts up about Jay, no one knows what to do or say. We just stand in the middle of the room, looking lost and tired.

Jay finally says, "Look outside. You can see the ocean and the beautiful beach from the living room through three big arches."

Rigo says, "Boss, what we do? I don't know where to look, what to touch. What the—"

"Rigo, grab me a beer and let's find out. Grab Jay a beer—I know he needs one!"

Rigo grabs some cold Indios and we walk out to the back porch, still stunned over all this wealth. We look out at the edge of the beach and can see a guy sitting alone, three empty chairs next to him.

Rigo looks out. "No way. Could that be...Toño?"

Wouldn't that be something.

"You think, boss? No way. Dude, that has to be him."

"Rigo, where's your cervesa? Go grab yourself one, and let's go find out."

We walk out from the porch onto the white sand. Is it him?

As we get closer, he turns like he can hear us. I can see he's smiling from his profile...Toño.

Toño is alive and sitting in a beach on the Yucatan Peninsula.

He stands up, wearing white shorts and an open white button-down shirt. How the hell did he get here? What's up with the palace and all this white shit?

And I thought we were in awe five minutes back. Seeing Toño takes the cake.

"Where's my knife?" he says casually.

I pull it out of my back pocket and hand it to him.

Toño smiles and with a father's voice says, "Ah, my baby. I missed you."

Next thing, we're laughing and yelling and there's hugs all around. If you haven't seen tough guys cry, well, then you haven't seen everything. Circling around and around yelling in two different languages. Maybe three—it sounds like some made up shit was in there, too. It was true love and relief. After fifteen minutes of that, Toño asks us to sit down. He has a story.

Of course he does.

18

THE GERMAN, PEPE IN CUERO TEXAS, 100 KILOS OF COKE, THE MEXICAN, AND EL COMMANDANTE

"The German is everything we thought he'd be—quick, smart, and to the point. They sat me down in front of a mahogany desk across from him. This guy is white-headed, with piercing blue eyes and a scar across his left cheek. He has this smooth, quiet demeanor with little, if any, expression on his face. Let me tell you, he was all business. He asks if I want anything to drink, to which I reply, 'A cold beer would be nice.' It's good for every occasion, even in the face of death. One of the guards goes to the bar and pours a beer in a plastic cup. This guy is good. What kind of damage can I cause with a fucking red Solo cup?"

"Shut up," Rigo interrupts. "Red Solo? Seriously, Toño."

"They make them in Mexico, pendejo. Now, can I tell the story?"

"Si, jefe."

I see Paco give Rigo a look to shut up—good luck with that. Then those happy eyes of his curl up at the edges. Shifting power can be tricky, but looks like we're all good. Paco looks like he is happy to drop back to second-in-command.

"So I down the beer in the red Solo and the German starts, 'Where is the girl?'"

"What do you say?"

"Rigo, we're gonna tape your mouth shut for two days if you don't stop," Jay says.

Another look from Paco shuts Rigo right up.

"I tell the German she is in Texas. 'Why is she there?' the German wants to know. 'To save our lives,' I say. Of course, he wants me to bring her to him. So I tell him I don't know where she is. If I did, we'd all be dead by now. The German stops and thinks."

I pause so they can stew on this.

"Then the German says, 'Good move. And I thought you were just another river rat. I must rethink this situation.'

At this point, I have to make my play and keep us from getting dead. 'The girl will be delivered to El Mesquite tomorrow, unharmed.' I promise him that. Then I let loose and tell him about my tio's plot. Then he tells me he knew all that, and asks again, 'Where is the girl?'"

"You have to like this guy—always on point," Rigo chuckles.

"The guards start edging toward me as to finish the job and move on. The German looks at them and nods. So I play the only chip I have left. 'I know where the 100 kilos are!' I say. The German stops the guards with a glance and asks, 'Where is this item?' I tell him I will take them to it, as to give me some value. I add that I'll get him the girl and the 100 kilos—all for a fair trade."

"What the hell, Toño—you were trying to barter with the German?"

"I say, 'Our lives in return, and our loyalty to the Mexican Cartel from here on out.' They know I'm of value, now. Still.... The German gets up and walks to another room. I'm sitting there, knowing it's a 50/50 shot I will make it out alive."

Damn, I need a drink just thinking about it. This Yucatan sun is brutal. Rigo is on his feet, grabbing me another cold Indio. I love my bros. Not only do they follow through on very thin plan, they deal in details. Rigo cracks it, hands it to me.

"The German returns to the desk. Oh, and let me tell you, he's wearing a really nice Canale suit. It's gray with a thin pinstripe. Normally, those guys are men in black, but not the German. What a rebel. He pulled it off, too. I should've opened with that, so you had the image sooner. Next time.

"Anyway, he smiles and sits down and says, 'I guess we are friends again, ay compadre. You take us to the kilos?' *Yes!* I shout—in my head, of course—and just nod. Then he says, 'You take us to the kilos and return the girl, and you and your crew get to stay alive, for now.' I agree, then add that I want a finder's fee and my tio's job."

"Toño!" Rigo almost splits in two laughing. "A fucking finder's fee? Really?"

"The German leans back and says, 'We will have to keep an eye on this one, ay boys. You get no finder's fee. But when and if it all works out, you will get a bonus.' Guys, I was shaking like a dog getting out of pond in December. They loaded me up in a two-car convoy, and off we go to Texas. What happened next was fucked up. We drive to Pepe's ranch, 200 miles away, without exchanging one word with these German mercs. We arrive at the ranch and it looks deserted. I start sweating bullets, knowing if Pepe or the dope aren't here, I'm gone to the dirt nap.

"Around the back was Pepe's Dodge 350 dually pickup. That was a godsend. I knew he was there, and one more chip fell my way. I was asked to wait in the car and keep

165

my mouth shut. All I heard was yelling and screaming for about twenty minutes. Then Pepe stumbles out of the ranch house, bleeding, with one of the German's Hitler Youth walking behind and giving him a push every couple of steps. They walk to the barn next to the main house. Next thing I hear is a shot. The mercs walk out with the coke in tow and load it in the second car.

"We drive off without saying a word. Course, I expected that at this point. No chitchat. The car with the coke goes north, and we drive back south to Laredo. These guys drove me 200 miles each way without saying a fucking word. Then they dropped me off at the Laredo Airport. They handed me my passport and my wallet, along with $1,000. Then these German fucks who haven't spoken in umpteen hours say, 'Welcome to slavery.' They smile and speed away.

"I stood by the statues of the American and Mexican cowboys outside the airport, thinking, *I can't believe I'm still alive.* Right then, I knew you guys had done the job, or I would have been left with Pepe in the barn as crow bait. I knew you guys would be on your way to Tulum. I grabbed some tacos at the airport and jumped on a plane to Cancun. I then took a taxi here to Pedro Paila and pre-pared for your arrival with all this jale. Not bad."

"Why this place?" Paco asks. "How the hell did you even know about this badass, first-class joint, Toño? It ain't never been on our radar."

"Remember when I told you guys a while back about the dude that owns that Island in the US/Canadian border? You remember—he introduced me to the governor of Monterrey last year."

Rigo nods. "Oh yeah, that blond dude with the million-dollar smile."

"That's right. His name is Peter, but that's another story I really can't even tell you guys. And you wouldn't believe me if I told you."

"So, Jefe, you outplayed the masters. I can't believe we are sitting here in Tulum, drinking beer on the beach."

"You look like a fucking angel, Toño. I almost started confessing when I saw you."

"Paco, I would never want to hear your confession. It would freak me out, 'specially what you did with that sheep."

"You're real funny, Toño. Real funny. Right now, I could care less, jefe."

"Boys, you guys did it. Like real pros, you did the things. You did good, Paco." Paco's head is hanging low. He's never been one for compliments.

"What now, Toño?" Rigo asks, changing the subject.

"Well, now we enjoy the ocean, get drunk, and eat. If you guys are still wanting to stick together as a crew, we start our new jobs as kings of South Texas when we return to the Valley. What comes next, we'll have to wait and see."

"I can't believe you sat with the German and lived to tell about it, vato."

"It worked out this time, Jay, but we have a job coming up when we get back. It's a piece of work that pays—makes this one look like chump change. Trickier, too. But hey, what else do we have to do?"

I don't have the heart to tell them Tio and El Machete are in the wind. My tio always has an escape plan—a Toyota truck one hundred yards from El Mesquite, pointing north toward the highway. When Commandante and Mexico's Suburbans arrived at El Mesquite, to whack them both, all they found was Machete's Cadillac and Tio's truck. Not a soul around. I wish I had been there to see the look on those pinche mercs' faces. Standing around with their thumb up their asses and a big grin to pass the humiliation of being a day late and a peso short, putos.

I wonder how my tio knew they were going to be hit that afternoon. I wonder about a lot of things as I stare into the faces of my friends and send a nod toward the perfect sky.

Thanks.

I hope my crew, my bros, didn't think we had all this luck without a little help. South Texas is a strange place for coincidences.

THE END

DICTIONARY

These translations can have different meanings in different parts of the world.

Chingado: Damn it

Que Paso: What's up

Jefita: Mom

Chante: Home, house

Refinar: Eat

Feria: Money

Tio: Uncle

Mirones: Onlookers, busybodies

Mesquite: Mesquite tree

Sal Si Puedes: Leave if you can

Monja: Nun

Compas: Friend

Machete: Machete, long blade

Pinsoyate: Dumbass, knucklehead

Esquina: Back up

Quetes: Guns, firearms

Fila: Knife

Tiros: Bullets

Gasofa: Vehicle gas

Huevos: Balls, guts

Pendejo: Stupid, idiot

Cuernos: Used to describe an AK-47

Vato and Ese: Guy, dude

Dale: Go on, let's do it, hurry up

Vales Verga: You ain't worth dick

Chingos: Many, a lot

Putas: Whores, prostitutes

Orale: Okay, it's cool

Virongas: Beers

Pinche: Cheap

Whachale: Watch out, look out

Gata Orcada: Strangled
cat
Baboso: Slobbering idiot
Mas Puta: The biggest
whore
Mijo: Son
Ya Vasta: That's enough
Apurate: Hurry
Abrasos: Hugs all around
Ruka: Girl, chick
Pachanga: Party, soiree
La Loma: The hill,
Juras: Cops, law enforce-
ment

Mamon: Sucker
Que Onda: What's up,
what's happening
Que Wato: What's going
on, what's up, what you
doing
Guey: Fool
Nombre: No way
Andale: Hurry
Comprendes:
Understand
Papeles: Papers, docu-
ments
Todo stupido: All stupid

ABOUT THE AUTHOR

TONY MOLINA was born in 1962 in Laredo, Texas. He lived in the small town of Zapata, Texas, where the setting of the novel was canvassed. Tony's debut novel captures the imagination  of the reader with intimate imagery and unique language. Tony became a police officer in Arlington, Texas. He spent thirteen years working with the SWAT team and four years as an undercover officer. His experience as a Vice and Narcotics Detective and SWAT member was invaluable in creating an intimate and authentic portrayal of the South Texas Drag way of life. He is now retired and living the dream, as they say.

SOUTH
TEXAS
DRAG